❧ **W9-AYF-593**

LEAD-PIPE CINCH

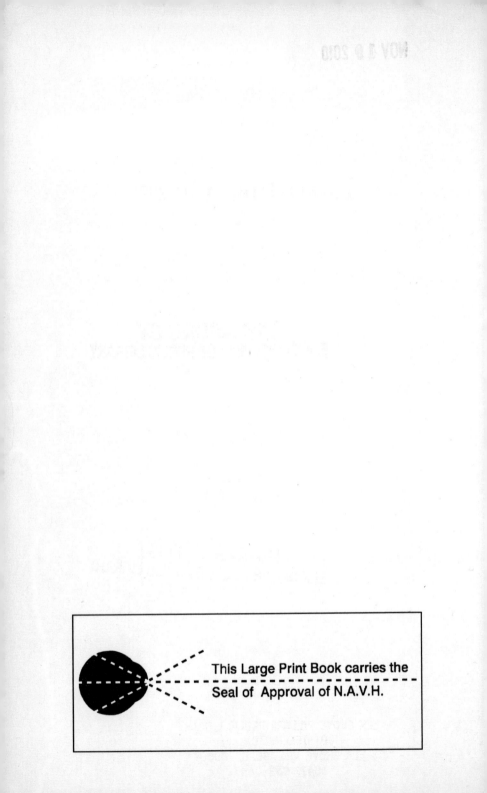

LEAD-PIPE CINCH

CHRISTY EVANS

WHEELER PUBLISHING
A part of Gale, Cengage Learning

Detroit • New York • San Francisco • New Haven, Conn • Waterville, Maine • London

GALE
CENGAGE Learning

LIBRARY OF CONGRESS CATALOGING-IN-PUBLICATION DATA

Evans, Christy.
　　Lead-pipe cinch / by Christy Evans.
　　　　p. cm. — (A Georgiana Neverall mystery) (Wheeler
　　Publishing large print cozy mystery)
　　ISBN-13: 978-1-4104-3047-2 (softcover)
　　ISBN-10: 1-4104-3047-2 (softcover)
　　　　1. Plumbers—Fiction. 2. Oregon—Fiction. 3. Large type
　　books. I. Title.
　　PS3605.V3647L43 2010
　　813'.6—dc22　　　　　　　　　　　　　　　　　　2010021658

Published in 2010 by arrangement with The Berkley Publishing Group, a member of Penguin Group (USA) Inc.

Printed in the United States of America
1 2 3 4 5 6 7 14 13 12 11 10

This one is for my mother,
who is nothing *like Sandra,*
and for Steve,
whose love and support makes
everything possible.

ACKNOWLEDGMENTS

The list is long, and my memory is short, but I want to thank everyone who helped make this book a reality:

Colleen, friend and first reader;

Denise and Michelle, fabulous editors;

Kris and Dean, mentors and friends who are there to talk me off the ledge when necessary;

Sheldon McArthur, the Yoda of crime fiction, and bookseller guru;

Jim, the "day job" boss who actually "gets it";

Pat and Shane, who trusted me enough to let me practice on their new vanity;

All my OWN buddies, for being a cheering section;

Especially to Cindie, for the coolest wrench ever;

And to Steve, my husband, best friend, and biggest fan. I hope you always feel that way.

CHAPTER 1

"Let's get a move on, Neverall," Sean Jacobs, the crew foreman, said as he gestured toward the muddy bottom of the trench. "The inspector's due in an hour."

Mud sucked at my boots as I slipped down the steep side of the troublesome McComb moat project, a shovel banging clumsily against my leg.

With permit hearings, never-ending inspections, and construction snafus, this job was fast becoming a plumber's nightmare.

The drainpipe we buried last week had to be uncovered this week. As the apprentice, I got all the bottom-of-the-barrel jobs. Or in this case, bottom of the moat.

We were supposed to be done before the rain started, but this year summer limited itself to a few weeks of clear skies and temperatures in the high nineties. Now it was only October, and the Great North-wet was already living up to its nickname.

I bit back a curse as the mud squished beneath my weathered steel-toed boots. No swearing on the job. It was one of the rules my boss, Barry Hickey, insisted upon. Barry had a lot of rules.

I reached the muck at the bottom of the six-foot-deep trench and checked the marker stakes. Buried beneath fourteen inches of dirt — now mud — was the pipe in question. It had to be uncovered and inspected — again — before the concrete lining could be poured.

This close to the recently erected bridge piers, the power equipment was useless. With the piers in place there was no room for a power shovel to maneuver. All this job required was a strong back and a lot of stubborn.

Sean and I had reached a truce of sorts. Although he still didn't believe a girl belonged on any kind of construction crew, after working together all summer I felt as though I was slowly earning his respect.

It was a familiar scenario. Several years in the boy's club of Silicon Valley high tech had taught me how to adapt. When I left behind the Union Square wardrobe and the hundred-hour workweeks, I had come away with some hard-earned lessons.

Not to mention a flattened bank account,

a bruised ego, and a broken heart — all courtesy of some of the slimier boys in the club.

By comparison, the thick mud at the bottom of the moat felt clean.

I shifted another shovelful of ooze, depositing it behind me. Water, dark with the rich soil, ran back down into the hole I'd created, obscuring the bottom.

I moved along the width of the moat, carefully uncovering a narrow trench. We would have to pump it dry for the inspector, but at least the rain had stopped. With luck, we could get the approval we needed and re-bury the pipe before the skies opened up again. The concrete, fortunately, would be someone else's problem.

Building a moat sounds simple. It's nothing more than a ditch, dug in a circle instead of a straight line. It was the stuff that went inside that circle that was the problem.

Power lines, cables, water lines, drainpipes — all the modern conveniences had to be fed to the McComb's castle — and had to run under the moat. It was one of the requirements of the permit. A local ordinance said *underground utilities.* That meant at least a foot of dirt over every pipe and cable, and we were sticking to the letter of the agreement.

It was a complex puzzle, feeding the latest technology to a state-of-the-art castle at the farthest reach of the grid. Three years ago, I would have been on the design team. As owner of Samurai Security, it was precisely the type of challenge I had looked for.

Instead I was up to my ankles in mud, dressed in stained coveralls and work boots. I was shoveling the muck, my hands protected by heavy leather gloves. I wore no jewelry, except a battered plastic wristwatch.

I was happier than I'd been in years.

Above me I heard a vehicle crunch to a stop on the gravel apron next to the bridge supports. I glanced at my watch with a sinking feeling. The inspector was half an hour early, and we were nowhere near ready.

"Hello, Mr. McComb," I heard Sean say, and I breathed a silent sigh of relief.

Chad McComb, the eccentric millionaire who wanted a castle and was willing to pay for it, was a welcome visitor at the job site. A retired Microsoft engineer who'd been hired so early in Microsoft's history that his employee number was rumored to be only two digits long, McComb treated the contractors and their crews well.

"Chad please, Sean." I could hear the

smile in McComb's voice. "How's the work going?"

Sean sighed. "Another blasted inspection. We're getting ready to pump out the rainwater. Inspector should be here in a few minutes."

"Won't keep you, then. Let me know if you need anything."

"Thanks, Mr. — Chad. I'll do that."

Footsteps rattled the boards over my head as McComb and a second person crossed the temporary bridge to the building site.

"Watch your step there, Blake," McComb said.

My heart did a little flip at the mention of his name, and I shook my head, disgusted with myself. There must be thousands of Blakes in the world, and Blake Weston was ancient history. So why, after three years, did I still react to the mention of his name? Just because I was thinking of the boy's club didn't mean a member of it was going to magically appear, like some evil sorcerer conjured out of my thoughts.

But before I could lift another shovelful of mud, I heard a voice that took my breath away as though I had been punched in the solar plexus.

Blake Weston's smooth voice, a rich baritone that used to give me goose bumps, answered McComb. "Certainly."

My veins were suddenly full of ice water. How could I be so sure, with only a single word? Maybe I just *thought* it sounded like *my* Blake. It had been three years, after all — just a coincidence.

Blake and McComb were looking at the building site in front of them, not at the muddy moat below, when I stepped away from the supports to look up.

I just had to look.

And I wished I hadn't.

The profile, the slick dark hair, the confident bearing, were all instantly familiar. It wasn't the power of suggestion, or a sound-alike, or some evil magic. It was Blake Weston.

I ducked back under the temporary bridge, forcing my attention back to the job at hand. With luck, I could stay in the moat, hidden from sight, until Blake and Mc-Comb left.

I strained to listen to their conversation, but they had moved away from the bridge.

"Ready for the pump?" Sean called down.

I froze, waiting for him to call me "Never-all," and reveal my presence to the last person on earth I wanted to see. But for once he didn't.

"Yep," I called back, pitching my voice

low, and hoping it wouldn't carry.

On the other hand, would Blake even recognize my voice? If he didn't, I wasn't sure whether I would be relieved or insulted. But the two men gave no indication they had heard our exchange.

A few minutes later, their footsteps muffled by the rhythmic thumping of the pump, Blake and McComb passed back across the temporary bridge and walked through the gravel.

Unable to resist, I clambered a few feet up the side of the moat, peeking over the rim of the trench. I had to confirm what I already knew.

One glance was all it took.

The first thing I saw from that vantage point was a pair of hand-stitched Italian loafers, now speckled with mud from their owner's trek through the construction site.

How appropriate. Blake Weston would never wear sneakers or work boots, even on a muddy construction site.

I hoped it was the last I would see of those despised loafers.

No such luck.

CHAPTER 2

I don't remember much of the rest of that morning. I know that we somehow got the moat pumped mostly dry, and the inspector came and went, shaking his head and muttering about crazy people. I hoped he meant the McCombs and their project, but it could have been me.

I wasn't at my best.

Of course, having a ghost rise up out of your past and walk by without seeing you can seriously mess up your day. But once I got over the initial shock, I wanted to know what Blake Weston, San Francisco man-about-town, was doing in Pine Ridge, Oregon?

And what was he doing dragging his expensive Italian loafers through the mud of a construction site? The man I knew, all too well, took a cab if the fog was thick and might leave condensation on his Burberry raincoat.

By the time I got off work, I was past curious and bordering on obsessive. I pulled my thirty-year-old Beetle into the driveway of my rental house without any sense of actually having driven anywhere. My mind was too full of Blake, and what he was doing here.

Daisy and Buddha, the Airedale parts of my family, met me at the door. They were anxious to visit the backyard, and I let them out before I stepped into the garage to strip out of my muddy coveralls.

I grabbed a clean T-shirt and jeans from the folded laundry and dashed for the bathroom, leaving the dirty coveralls in a heap. I'd take care of them later, but first I really wanted to be clean and dry and warm.

I stepped out of the shower and towel-dried my short hair. Low-maintenance wardrobe, low-maintenance hair, low-maintenance car. I was learning to love my whole low-maintenance life.

It was a far cry from the always-on-call, dry-clean only, high-maintenance lifestyle I'd had in San Francisco, and I liked it a lot.

I always thought better on my feet with a leash in my hand. As soon as Daisy and Buddha saw me take the leashes off the hook by the door, they were ready to go.

Soon we were on our way into the dusky evening, the dogs sniffing at all kinds of interesting bushes and weeds and me deep in thought.

We made our nightly two-mile circuit, Daisy straining against the leash in her usual impatient fashion, and Buddha walking serenely. Although the dogs were littermates with the same obedience training and home, their personalities mirrored their names. I swore I would never again name a dog after a flighty fictional heroine. Who knew what might happen if I named a dog Scarlett?

But speculating about dog names wasn't enough to distract me from the real problem. What was Blake Weston doing in Pine Ridge, and why was he at the McComb construction site today?

I didn't trust Blake. Not after the role he played in the destruction of Samurai Security. No one in Pine Ridge knew why I'd come back from San Francisco, and I intended to keep it that way. But Blake's presence could make it difficult to keep my secret.

I would have to steer clear of him as much as possible, and hope he would be gone soon. It wasn't much of a plan, but it was all I could come up with for now. If I knew what he was up to I might be able to build a better program, but for now this would have to do.

My cell phone rang, and I glanced at the lighted display, pleased to see the number of my best friend, Sue Gibbons.

"Dinner?" Sue said without preamble when I answered. "Tiny's?"

"Give me fifteen minutes," I panted. "I'm walking the dogs, and we're still a few blocks from home. Meet you there?"

I hurried the dogs home, gave them each one of their favorite green treats, and grabbed my purse.

Tiny's was about a five-minute drive. In a town the size of Pine Ridge, most everything was a five-minute drive from everything else. Another low-maintenance option.

It was an option I was learning to enjoy, after the years of Bay Area traffic followed by several months of Portland gridlock. It meant I didn't have the luxury of hundreds of shopping, dining, and entertainment options, but Portland was less than an hour away when I needed a "big city" fix.

To my mind, it was the best of both worlds.

I pulled the Beetle into Tiny's graveled parking lot and looked around to see which cars I recognized. Sue's SUV was parked at the front of the lot, and there were a couple of rigs I recognized from the various construction sites I'd worked on over the summer.

I didn't spot Wade's hybrid sedan, and I felt a guilty rush of relief. I was far too preoccupied with Blake Weston, and what he was doing in Pine Ridge, to deal with my sometime-boyfriend, City Councilman Wade Montgomery.

I walked through the door, stopping to let my eyes adjust to the dim light of the tavern.

Tiny's was a neighborhood watering hole that had been here as long as I could remember. When I was a kid, it was a mysterious place where only the grown-ups were allowed, and we all yearned to see what was inside.

Now I knew it was just a local tavern with stools covered in brittle red vinyl, mismatched chairs, and scarred wooden tables. It smelled of beer and hot grease, and served the best chicken fingers I'd ever tasted.

Sue waved to me from a table near the so-called dance floor — a few square feet of light-colored wood set into the dark floorboards, with an old-fashioned jukebox next to it. Friday and Saturday nights there might be a few couples dancing, but tonight the floor was deserted.

She hooked a thumb in the direction of the bar. "Figured you wanted chicken and microbrew," she said, "so I already ordered for us."

I nodded my agreement. Sue knew me well. "How much do I owe you?"

She shook her head. "I had a good day, you can catch it next time."

I gave her a wide-eyed look. "It must have been good for you to pick up a check, Gibbons. What gives?"

She chuckled. "What, you don't think I can pick up a check now and again? I am wounded, I tell you. Wounded."

"I helped you set up your computer, remember? Got the bookkeeping program running? I've seen your bank accounts, woman. I know you're not exactly rolling in dough."

She nodded. She was one of the few people in Pine Ridge who'd seen what I could do with a computer. My boss, Barry Hickey, was another. Mostly, however, I'd left that part of my life in San Francisco and I didn't talk about it.

"So, what does *a good day* mean at Doggy Day Spa?"

Sue grinned, relishing the delay. "I have a new regular," she said, "and she tips well!"

"Really? Who?"

"Astrid McComb. Remember I told you she brought in an adorable Yorkie a couple weeks back?"

I nodded.

"Well, today she showed up with the Yorkie again — said he just loved coming to see me." She preened a little, then continued, "But she also had a pair of Old English sheepdog puppies. Said she thought they were more appropriate for the castle."

"That's one way to choose a dog, I suppose," I said, sarcasm dripping.

"It's not like that," Sue said. "She was looking for another dog, and she fell in love with these two. Couldn't decide between them, so she got 'em both.

"Anyway," she continued, "she brought them both in for grooming today and told me she wanted a standing appointment every week."

"Nice."

"Even better was the tip she left. More than paid for tonight's dinner." She paused and glanced back at the bar. "Which, by the way, looks like it's ready."

Katie, the barmaid, brought the steaming baskets to our table along with a couple frosty mugs of microbrew. I felt the heat radiating from the food, and quickly decided I could give it a few minutes to cool down.

Sue looked at me, wiping a drop of foam from her lip. "You installed that tracking program, but I still don't understand what it really does. Can we go over that again?"

Sue's conversations were often a roller-coaster ride of subject changes and non sequiturs. Her thoughts raced ahead of her words, and she dove headlong into a new subject without transition.

This time she'd done a U-turn, back to her computer system. A few months earlier I had cleaned up some software issues, and put tracking and security software in place. I'd given her the Samurai Security standard instruction lecture when I was finished, but she still had a lot to learn.

I launched into an explanation of what the various programs did, but I dialed it back within a couple minutes, as I saw her eyes glaze over. "Sorry," I said. "Sometimes I forget I don't do that anymore."

Sue eyed me with a troubled look. "Yeah, but you sure sound like you still could. Why don't you? It's got to be a heckuva lot more lucrative than being a plumber."

"Apprentice plumber," I corrected, trying to steer the conversation away from my previous profession. "I still have more than a year before I can get my certification. And that is assuming I even pass the exams."

Sue rolled her eyes. "You, worried about exams? Puhleeese, Miss Graduated-From-One-of-the-Toughest-Schools-on-the-Planet. You can pass any exam you want."

I shrugged. "Maybe so." To tell the truth, I was proud of the computer science degree from Caltech, and the math and science *did* help with some of my plumbing class work.

But I had learned the hard way that nothing guaranteed success — in academic affairs, or business affairs.

Which brought me back to Blake, and his presence in Pine Ridge.

Why was he here?

CHAPTER 3

Unfortunately, I was about to get an answer from the inimitable Mr. Weston himself.

Not that I expected to see Blake in a local dive like Tiny's. He should have been in Portland at a white-tablecloth restaurant with an impressive wine list, not at a tavern where every dish starts with *fried* and the beverage choices are bottle or draft.

Yet there he was, walking through the door of Tiny's with Chad and Astrid McComb, the three of them yakking like old friends.

I searched my memory, wondering if Blake had ever mentioned Chad or Astrid. However, most of what I remembered of my conversations with Blake centered around Samurai Security — or topics I couldn't think about without cringing — and I didn't remember any reference to the McCombs.

"Earth to Neverall," Sue said, snapping her fingers in my face. "You still with us,

Georgie?"

I turned to look back at Sue. She was staring at me, her forehead furrowed with concern. "Are you okay? You look like you've seen a ghost."

I shook my head. "I'm fine. Really." I picked up my beer and took a sip to cover my distraction.

I felt as if I was being watched, and not by Sue. Did I really think Blake Weston even remembered my name five minutes after I fled San Francisco, much less three years later? Not likely.

"Who's the hunk?" Sue asked, glancing behind me.

"What hunk?" I stalled, pretending I didn't know exactly who she was talking about.

"The one with Astrid and her husband," she replied. "The one that's checking you out."

"Likely story," I said. "Nobody checks out anybody in Tiny's. You've got this place confused with the Meet Market." I named the singles' hangout a few miles west. "That's where you go to check people out."

"Yeah? Well, he's definitely headed this way."

"Maybe he's checking you out," I said. "Ever think of that?" I leaned over my food, wishing my hair was long enough to hide my face, but the practical low-maintenance cut left me exposed.

Sue shook her head. "Definitely focused on you," she said.

I refused to turn around. I knew who it was. What was I going to say? Hi, Blake. How've you been since you stole my business and destroyed my life?

And how would I explain him to the people around me? I had left my high-tech life behind, had buried it and started over. It was history — dead and gone — and I wanted it to stay that way.

"Gee?" The voice sent goose bumps across my arms, the nickname all too familiar. "Gee, is that really you?" The incredulous tone, slightly superior, mocked me. "What are you doing here?"

Chad McComb appeared in my field of vision, edging around the side of our small table. "Georgiana?" he said tentatively. "This is Blake Weston, a colleague of mine from the Bay Area?" His voice rose at the end of his sentence, as though he was unsure how to introduce Blake.

"Perhaps you've met?" Chad sounded puzzled.

I turned slowly in my chair, aware of Sue watching my every move. There would be awkward questions later. I shoved the thought to the back of my mind, and tried to concentrate.

My lizard brain — the uncontrolled panic center that runs on pure emotion — screamed at me to run. Knock over the chair, run like hell, and put as much distance as possible between me and the taunting ghost of my old life.

Instead, I forced myself to look up at Blake with as blank a stare as I could manage. "Blake Weston? I used to know someone by that name."

The face was the same. The self-satisfied smirk was exactly as I remembered from the last time I'd seen him, and it didn't slip a millimeter. There was no mistaking the man who had stolen my company, and he knew it.

I held his gaze. No more running. "Blake." I nodded. "It's been a long time."

Not long enough, the lizard brain screamed. I ignored it.

"Gee, nice to see you," Blake lied. The last time we had spoken, he'd made it clear he never wanted to see me again.

"What brings you to Pine Ridge?" I asked politely. I hoped he'd answer quickly and then go away.

But judging by the sneer that passed for a

smile, he was enjoying my discomfort. "I'm consulting with Chad, here" — he clapped McComb on the shoulder as though they were old friends — "on the security issues for his new place.

"You know how it goes. Someone asks for your help, you do what you can." He shrugged with false modesty. "I'm just here to help for a few days."

The expression on Chad's face said there was more to the visit than Blake was telling me. I told myself I didn't care.

"Georgiana's working on the house, Blake," Chad offered. "She's part of the plumbing crew that's trying to solve the moat issues. Barry tells me she's invaluable."

I held my breath. My plumbing skills weren't enough to make me stand out, and I had sworn Barry to secrecy about the computer skills that had made me so valuable. He wouldn't violate my trust, would he?

Chad stopped and looked from me to Blake and back again.

Blake gave me a wolfish grin. "You're working as a plumber?" he asked with barely concealed glee.

I nodded. This was getting worse by the minute.

Sue came to my rescue. "How are the dogs, Astrid?"

Astrid brightened at the mention of her beloved pets. "Angus is getting used to the new pups," she said. "And they are adjusting to him. In fact, just yesterday —"

"I, uh, we should let these two eat, before their food gets cold," Chad cut in. He took Astrid's elbow to steer her away from our table.

"See you out at the site, Georgie," he said, nodding to me. He turned to Blake. "Shall we?"

Blake smirked at me with an expression that made it clear our conversation was far from over.

As soon as they were out of earshot, Sue exploded. "Who was that?!"

"Just somebody I used to work with."

She snorted. "And that's why you're falling apart just saying hello? I don't think so." She leaned forward and crossed her arms on the table. "Let's try again, Neverall. Who was that?"

"You heard Chad," I evaded. "His name is Blake Weston."

Sue rolled her eyes. "And who is Blake Weston? And don't you dare tell me he's just somebody you used to work with. I'm not buying it."

I sighed. I was going to have to confess something.

CHAPTER 4

"It's a long story."

"I have all night," Sue said.

"I'm waiting," she singsonged when I didn't immediately respond.

I hesitated, unsure how much it would take to satisfy her.

Sue continued to stare at me.

She wasn't going to let me off the hook.

"We had a, uh, relationship. It ended badly."

"And . . . ?"

I fiddled with the cold fries in my basket, breaking one into little pieces and dropping them back into the basket. "And nothing. I left San Francisco and I haven't seen him since."

"Until tonight," Sue added.

"Not exactly." The words blurted out before I could stop myself. Relief flashed through me, surprising me with the intensity of the emotion.

Sue's eyes widened. "When did you see him?"

I glanced around, making sure no one was within eavesdropping distance. "This morning," I whispered. "He was at the job site."

"He didn't recognize you?" Her voice was incredulous. "That's a *really* bad breakup."

"He didn't see me. I was down in the moat when he got there, and I stayed there." I couldn't meet her gaze while I talked, but it was comforting to unload some of the burden I had carried for the last three years.

Sue reached across the table and patted my arm. "You don't have to tell me, Georgie."

The sympathy in her voice touched me, and I gripped her hand. Hard. "Thanks, Sue. I, um, I have to think about this. But maybe sometime soon . . ."

I released Sue's hand, and let the emotion of the moment pass. It would come back, I knew. Just like Blake.

Running into Blake had taken the fun out of the evening. I abandoned my dinner, my appetite gone, and said good night to Sue. She nodded her understanding, and made me promise to call her the next day.

I walked out of Tiny's, trying to ignore the feeling of being watched. My knees threatened to give out, but I kept walking. I would not let Blake know he'd gotten to me.

On the way home the full impact of Blake's words sank in. He was *consulting* on the security measures for the McComb's castle. A job I would have had.

I thought back to everything that had been said. Chad had introduced Blake as a colleague, not a friend. It explained why Blake had never mentioned him — especially if he figured there might be future business to steal, along with my company.

By the time I pulled my old Bug into the driveway, I had convinced myself it was just a nasty coincidence, and if I just kept out of Blake's path for a few days it would all be over.

I locked the car, more from force of habit than from any security concern. It wouldn't take much to jimmy the thirty-year-old lock, if anyone was really crazy enough to want a beat-up relic.

By the time I reached the McComb site in the morning, the skies had cleared, and pale October sunlight filtered through the tall evergreens.

The Bug was the first car in the parking area. I sat behind the wheel, sipping black coffee out of a take-out cup from Dee's

Lunch on Main Street.

A flight of Canada geese passed overhead, their harsh calls a vivid reminder of why they were nicknamed honkers. I climbed out of the car to watch their progress as they grew smaller and their cries faded in the distance. It was a sure sign of the cold weather to come.

I leaned against the car and looked over the site. I tried to imagine how it would look when it was finished, though I had only seen a few rough sketches of the McCombs's plans.

The island we were creating was about a half acre of bare dirt and rocks, with a copse of small oaks near the center. From the plans, I knew they planned to keep the trees as the starting point for a central garden.

Designing the irrigation and drainage for the garden was going to be a challenge. Barry had hinted that my programming skills could be applied to the project. There were parallels, and I had to admit it had its appeal. I was already leaning on Barry to invest in some design software.

He was resisting, but I counted on the gentle persuasion of a valued client with an open wallet to convince him. That project was several months down the road, and for now we had to concentrate on the moat.

Unless we could make that work, the rest of the project would never happen.

In the distance I heard vehicles approaching, the rumble of engines disturbing the morning solitude. In a few minutes, Sean's pickup pulled into the gravel parking area followed by two more vehicles.

Time to get to work.

Burying the newly inspected pipe — again — took most of the morning. Once again, as the apprentice, I was at the bottom of the moat with a shovel.

Midway through the morning I heard tires crunching in the gravel above me — probably Barry coming to inspect the job. I set aside my shovel and scrambled for the top of the moat.

I reached the edge and looked over, expecting to see Barry's boots.

Hand-stitched Italian loafers.

Blake.

I started to duck back into the moat, but that familiar mocking tone caught me.

"Gee? Is that you down there?"

Behind him I saw Sean mouth "Gee?"

"Yes, Blake." I tried to keep my voice neutral.

I clambered out of the moat and stood up on the edge of the trench. "Is there something I can do for you?"

"I wanted to come back out and take another look at the site. Without the client, of course."

He chuckled, a nasty sound that grated at my already-shredded nerves. "You remember how that is," he said, reaching out to touch my arm. "Don't you?"

I fought back the impulse of the lizard brain, refusing to shrink from his touch. I bit hard on the inside of my bottom lip, focusing on the pain rather than Blake.

When I was sure I could answer without my voice faltering, I replied. "That was a long time ago, Blake."

"Not that long, Gee." His voice slid across me, making my skin crawl.

I figured I had held my ground long enough. I pulled back and stepped away.

Over Blake's shoulder I saw Sean move closer. He was watching us, his body language clearly protective.

I shook my head a fraction of an inch, hoping he understood. I could handle this by myself.

"What do you want, Blake? I'm working here. I don't have time to play games with you."

By now we had an audience. The entire crew had stopped working, though they tried to cover up their interest.

"Then go back to work, Gee. You know I can handle this just fine without you." He looked down into the trench, then back at me in my muddy coveralls. "You seem to have found an, um, interesting place to work."

He turned his back, dismissing me.

Anger flashed over me. Adrenaline shot through my system, sending my heart racing and spiking my body heat.

I would not allow him to dismiss me again.

Not here.

Not now.

"Blake, you lying, thieving low-life son of a —" I bit back the last word. I hadn't completely forgotten where I was.

He turned back, eyebrows raised. "Do you have a problem, Gee? Your temper always was one of your least attractive features."

I swallowed hard. I had spent many years of martial arts training learning to control that temper. Blake wasn't worth surrendering to it again.

"No," I said slowly. "No problem." I turned and climbed down into the moat.

I didn't look back.

I reached the bottom of the moat, picked up my shovel, and went back to work. Above me I heard the murmur of voices and the clank of tools as the crew returned to their jobs.

I focused on my movements, falling into the rhythm and repetition.

I let the adrenaline and emotion drain away, replaced with my hard-learned calm. It wasn't easy. I still wanted to climb out of the moat and scream at Blake. I wanted to strike back, to wipe that self-satisfied smirk from his face.

I wouldn't do it. Nothing would bring back the company I had built, or the life I had led.

And, really, did I even want that life back?

Despite my resolve, however, I listened for movement above. For a few minutes all I heard were the normal sounds of the crew at work. No one approached Blake, or spoke to him, and he didn't speak to anyone.

I could picture him, standing where I had left him, looking down on the crew both figuratively and literally.

Blake was a couple inches over six feet and distance-runner slender. Combined with his posture and attitude, you always had the feeling he was looking at you from a great distance — strange that I had never noticed that before.

I waited.

Eventually, after several minutes that felt

like hours, I heard his footsteps move across the gravel parking area. A car door slammed, and the engine of the luxury rental purred to life — only the best for Blake Weston.

Even when it was paid for by the company he stole from me.

CHAPTER 5

A couple minutes later, Sean's head appeared over the lip of the moat.

"Coast's clear, Neverall."

I handed him the shovel and climbed out of the trench.

"Sorry for the disruption."

He shook his head. "No problem," he said, unconsciously echoing my own words. He hesitated, then added, "Some men can be jerks, too."

He walked away before I could answer.

It was as close as we had come to a friendly exchange. Sean had, as they say, issues with women. In an argument, he'd side with the man every time.

At first I had labeled him a *troglodyte,* and let it go at that. But Wade had explained it to me several months ago. Sean's marriage had crumbled, and in a town the size of Pine Ridge there were no secrets. Everyone knew of the other woman — hers, not his.

Coming from Sean, this exchange was practically admission to his boy's club, and I was grateful for how far our relationship had come. We might never be buddies, but we could work together.

And I could trust Sean, unlike *some* people I had worked with.

I took a couple deep breaths. Let it go, Neverall.

By the time I climbed into the Bug and headed home, I had put the confrontation with Blake behind me. He was history, and I never wanted to see him again.

Be careful what you wish for.

I parked at the curb, leaving the driveway empty. I was expected at my mother's for dinner in an hour, and I always took my other car when I visited my mother.

She hated my other car.

When I left San Francisco the Jimmy Choos went to a consignment shop along with the Fendi bags, and the Union Square wardrobe was donated to Dress to Succeed, a woman's shelter program.

I shipped Daisy and Buddha north in comfort, gave away my furniture, and drove back to Portland with only what would fit in my "toy."

I'd bought the candy-apple red vintage

Corvette the day I cashed my first stock options. It was a visible symbol that I had made it. Eighteen months later I was broke and unemployed, but I stubbornly clung to the Corvette.

The Bug had been a graduation gift from my dad, and I'd left it stored in his garage — a triumph of sentiment over logic for many years — until I moved back to Pine Ridge.

Now the Bug was much more practical than the convertible, and the roles were reversed. The 'Vette lived in the garage, taken out only for special occasions, such as a sunny afternoon drive on the sweeping mountain curves of Mount Hood.

Or to annoy my mother.

I rolled into her driveway with the rumble of 427 well-tuned cubic inches, and goosed the throttle just once before shutting off the engine.

She appeared at the door just as I emerged from the driver's seat, her carefully lipsticked mouth set in a tight line. It was her what-will-the-neighbors-think expression. I didn't need to tell her that I really didn't much care what the neighbors thought.

But she cared.

I was early. The garage door stood open, Mom's Escalade parked to one side. The other side stood empty. All my growing-up years it had held a late-model Chrysler, my father's idea of the perfect car for the town doctor. A month after he died, the last Chrysler was repossessed by the bank.

My mother, his widow, discovered one reason the beloved Doctor Neverall was so beloved. It seems when the local economy turned sour, he stopped billing his uninsured patients, which included most of the town of Pine Ridge.

She held on to the house through a combination of insurance payments and a balancing act worthy of the Flying Wallendas. My meager savings were tied up in Samurai Security, and I couldn't help her. By the time I could, she had discovered how to take care of herself.

The Escalade was both a business necessity and a status symbol. Sandra Neverall transformed herself from doctor's widow to one of the top producers at Whitlock Estates Realty and a good friend of the owner, Gregory Whitlock.

A very good friend.

The empty space in the garage was for him.

Forcing my thoughts from the too-smooth Gregory, I locked the 'Vette and crossed the lawn to the front door.

I was spared the awkwardness that came every time I approached the house. I had once lived there and gone in and out at will. Now I was a guest and if mom wasn't waiting at the door, I knocked and waited for an invitation to enter.

I wasn't spared the disapproving frown that told me she had heard the throaty roar of the 'Vette's engine. She pulled me in for an obligatory hug as I crossed the threshold. I knew she was scowling over my shoulder at my inappropriate car when her arms went around me.

"Georgiana," she said, releasing me and holding me at arm's length, "I'm so glad you didn't dress up. This is just a quiet family dinner, after all."

It wasn't a compliment. Mom believed a woman should always look her best, and that included fresh makeup and every hair in place. My wool slacks and cashmere sweater made the grade, barely. As for the rest of me, below par.

"Come in the kitchen," she said. "I'm just finishing up dinner."

I followed obediently. After thirty-plus years I had given up trying to refuse her commands. Once upon a time I thought I would outgrow her power. Now I knew better.

I fell into my usual kitchen tasks, setting the table and arranging the vegetable tray, as Mom chattered on about her latest real estate triumphs, with regular references to Gregory.

Mom prided herself on serving a home-cooked meal every night. If she was home alone she had tidy containers of leftovers, each one calculated to be exactly the right amount for one person. They stacked neatly in her freezer and she was careful to use them in date order.

I wasn't completely helpless in the food department myself. I had the best pizza place in town on my speed dial.

Mom placed deviled eggs in a specially designed plate. "You like deviled eggs, don't you? They're Gregory's favorite, you know."

I hated egg salad, and deviled eggs were just egg salad with less chopping, but I didn't bother to contradict her. After all, they were Gregory's favorite.

I heard Gregory's Mercedes pull into the garage. The diesel engine rumbled for a moment, then quieted. In a minute the back door opened. Gregory let himself in without knocking.

"Something smells good," he said, before wrapping one long arm around Mom and kissing her lightly on the cheek.

I kept my eyes on my work, careful not to actually look at the two of them. I heard Mom say something very quietly. Though I couldn't make out the actual words, from the corner of my eye I saw Gregory pull away from her.

The message was clear. Not in front of her daughter.

I bit my tongue. It had become clear several months ago that Gregory was sleeping with my mother. I didn't want to know then and I still didn't want to know now, but I did.

I tried not to think about it.

Gregory came to look over my shoulder. "Veggie tray, huh?"

I held back the sarcastic response that waited on the tip of my tongue, and nodded. "Be ready in just a minute."

We were all saved by the sound of the doorbell. I abandoned the veggies. "I'll get it."

Wade was right on time, his sensible hybrid a silent reproach parked next to my 'Vette. Wade grinned at me as he came through the door. "Annoying your mother again?" He glanced toward the driveway.

I laughed. Wade knew me better than I cared to admit. I gave him a quick hug of greeting. "Mom and Gregory are in the kitchen. Dinner should be just about ready."

I took Wade's Gore-Tex jacket and hung it in the hall closet. "Go sit down," I said, pointing him toward the living room. "I'll send Gregory in to keep you company."

I passed Gregory in the dining room on my way back to the kitchen. He carried the deviled-egg plate. Two depressions were already empty and there was a suspicious spot of yellow at the corner of his mouth.

He lowered his voice to a conspiratorial whisper. "Sandy makes the best deviled eggs in the state. Want one before they're gone?"

No one, even my father, ever called my mother Sandy — Sandra, or Mrs. Neverall, or Georgie's mom, but not Sandy. It took some getting used to.

I shook my head. "No thanks."

"Don't know what you're missing."

I heard Wade greet Gregory as I went through the kitchen door. Although I wouldn't exactly call the two men friends, they were cordial.

Wade's political ambitions went well beyond the Pine Ridge City Council. Gregory had supported his campaign, and Wade expected his continued support as he moved up the local political ladder.

I steered the dinner conversation into neutral channels as much as possible. We

48

chatted our way through the pork roast and baked potatoes, speculating on the high school football team's chances this season (good), the new television season (poor), and whether the bond measure for the community center would pass (doubtful).

We made it to dessert before it all fell apart.

I was carrying in the apple pie — which I suspected Mom had bought from Dee's Lunch even if she would never admit it — when Gregory dropped his bombshell.

"So, Georgiana, I hear there was some excitement out at the McComb site this morning."

I managed to get the pie on the table without breaking the dish, my heart pounding.

He looked up at me, his face a study in innocence. But there was something in his eyes, a look that made me wonder just how much he knew about Blake Weston.

I kept my voice steady as I answered. "A pretty normal day — for that project. Nothing's easy when you're building a moat."

"I'll bet," Wade chimed in. He obviously wasn't getting the undercurrent between Gregory and me.

"I heard it was a little more than that."

Gregory's voice reminded me of Blake's — a little too smooth for me.

I shrugged.

"I heard you had a visitor," he pressed. "Wondered what all the commotion was about."

I refused to get upset as I had earlier in the day. Gregory was pushing, but I could control myself.

I passed Gregory a piece of pie, then handed one to Mother, and finally one to Wade. Wade's expression showed his concern, but he waited, letting me handle the situation.

The boy was learning.

"Actually, Gregory," I said as I sat back down, "it was just the security consultant McComb hired."

"But he was someone you know?"

"*Used* to know," I corrected. "A long time ago."

I shot Wade a smile I hoped was reassuring, and focused my attention on Mom. She looked uncomfortably aware of the touch of hostility in Gregory's questioning.

"So, Mom, what was it you were saying earlier about the Clackamas Commons project? You had some new sales projections?"

We moved back to safer subjects, but I was left with a lingering unease. Why had Gregory been so intent on discussing Blake Weston's visit to the job site? And why bring it up in the middle of dinner?

CHAPTER 6

My mother had the same questions.

She motioned for me to help her clear the dessert dishes and follow her into the kitchen. She immediately closed the door behind us.

"What was that all about?" she demanded. "Do you have any idea how embarrassing it is to have Gregory know more about your life than your own mother does?"

Now that was more like it. For an instant I'd thought she was worried about me. But no, she was worried about how it made her look.

Be fair, I reasoned. She knows I can take care of myself, and I've deliberately kept her out of my life because she doesn't agree with the choices I've made.

It wasn't that my mother thought a husband and family were a better choice than an advanced degree. She thought they were the *only* choice.

The arguments ran through my head, an instant replay of our every conversation. She thought college — especially one with a high male to female ratio — was a way to earn a "Mrs." I was proud of my MS. It was a fundamental difference.

Still, she loved me, and I loved her in spite of our differences.

I touched her arm. "It was just someone I knew a long time ago, Mom. Someone I hoped I would never see again. He was a jerk. I'd almost forgotten about him," I lied smoothly, "until he showed up here."

"Well," she didn't sound convinced, but she seemed willing to cut me some slack. "If you say so." She gave me a sharp look. "You'd tell me if it was more than that, wouldn't you, Georgiana? I mean, I *am* your mother."

I sighed. "Of course I would." Another lie, but a necessary one if I wanted to put an end to this conversation. "But there's nothing to tell. Really."

Mom walked past me toward the kitchen door. She stopped and gave me a stiff hug. Then, as though embarrassed by the moment, she pulled away and walked quickly back into the dining room.

I sighed again. She drove me nuts, and we disagreed about nearly everything, but she

was still my mother. We were all we had —
if I didn't count Gregory, which I didn't —
and we were stuck with each other.

I was sure there were worse things.

I was about to find out how true that was.

By morning I had put Gregory and his odd
behavior out of my mind. He had certainly
been in a strange mood, but that was his
problem, not mine. Who knows? Maybe he
saw me as a threat to his relationship with
my mother.

Not that I had any intention of interfering
in Sandra Neverall's love life. I preferred to
stay as far away from *that* subject as possible.

My own track record wasn't anything to
brag about, after all. Before the Blake
debacle there were several years of a social
life that consisted primarily of study groups,
the occasional Ptomaine Tommy's burger
run, and the annual liquid nitrogen frozen
pumpkin drop. And while Ditch Day had
its social aspects, it was practically a civic
duty. Not a serious romantic relationship in
the bunch.

I'd dated Wade for a few months in high
school, and my mother had harbored high
hopes for our future together. He was smart
and ambitious, and she still considered him

a very acceptable choice.

She never understood why we broke up, and I hadn't tried to explain. I mean, how do you explain dumping an otherwise nice guy because he didn't rat out his buddy for cheating on your best friend? I ranted about his complicity to my friends — I was as dramatic as any teenager, albeit with a better vocabulary — but never to my mother.

Sue had found out about the jerk on her own, dumped him, and become the first prom queen to show up without a date. My relationship with Wade had never recovered.

Now we were dating again, trying to figure out if there was still something between us.

I was beginning to believe there was, though Wade had occasional doubts; like the time a few months earlier when he'd almost caught Sue and me breaking into Martha Tepper's house. Sure, we'd been trying to catch a thief and a murderer — and we'd been right — but having a cat burglar for a girlfriend was a definite detriment to a political career.

The skies were gray and a heavy fog clung to the highway as the Beetle chugged up the final hill to the McComb site. It was going to be a lousy day to work outside: cold and clammy, the daylight deadened by the low-hanging clouds. It had rained during the night, and there would be water standing in the bottom of the moat.

I wasn't looking forward to the day's work.

As I neared the top I heard idling engines and male voices carrying through the still morning. I wasn't always the first one on the site, but I was usually early, and I cherished those quiet moments before the crew arrived.

It was a habit I'd developed at Samurai Security. Arriving before my employees had allowed me uninterrupted time, a rarity in the hard-driving high-tech world. Yet Blake had somehow managed to turn even that against me in the final days.

I shook off the memory. Blake was history. Period.

When I topped the rise, emerging on the plateau where the site looked down on the surrounding pine forest, the sky was lit with red-and-blue strobe lights.

In the middle of the gravel pad an ambulance idled, puffs of exhaust creating vapor clouds in the cold morning air. The sheriff's cruiser was parked a few feet away, its bubble gum machine strobing in counterpoint to the lights on the ambulance.

For one surreal moment I realized this must have been how my parents' house looked the night my father had his heart attack.

Then reality hit me. There were rescue crews on our job site. Someone on the crew was hurt, badly enough to call an ambulance.

I slammed on the brakes and jumped from the car. I had to find out who was hurt, had to help if I could.

My heart raced as I ran toward the edge of the trench. If someone was hurt, I knew it would be in the moat.

Maybe it wasn't that bad.

Maybe it was just a false alarm.

Maybe they didn't need the ambulance after all.

A deputy stood in my path, and I tried to run around him. His arm reached out as I passed, snagging the sleeve of my Windbreaker.

"Not so fast, ma'am. No one's allowed up there." He nodded toward the site, where I could see uniformed men milling about.

"I work here," I snapped.

"Don't think anybody's working today," the deputy said, releasing my sleeve. "You might as well go back home."

"That's kind of up to my boss." I checked his name plate. "Don't you think so, Deputy Wheeler?"

"Who's your boss?" he asked slowly.

"Uh, Barry. Barry Hickey. Hickey & Hickey Plumbing?"

The deputy eyed me up and down. My coveralls were relatively clean, and I'd brushed off my boots, but I was sure I looked the part.

"I'm on the plumbing crew," I added.

The deputy didn't respond, and my imagination started working overtime. Maybe Barry was hurt, and he wasn't going to tell me.

"Tell me what's going on."

The deputy hesitated before he answered. "There's been an accident. This site is closed while we investigate. No one will be working here today, so, as I said, you might as well go home."

"Is someone hurt, Deputy Wheeler? I know all the guys on the crew. Who is it?"

Wheeler pressed his lips into a thin line. Obviously, he didn't intend to tell me anything more.

I debated my options. There weren't many. Wheeler was broad-chested, and his arms strained the sleeves of his uniform jacket.

I couldn't push past him, and I couldn't see around him, but I wasn't going away.

"Miss Neverall?"

58

I heard Sheriff Mitchell's voice from behind the deputy. As he loomed out of the fog, his face became recognizable.

"What are *you* doing here?" It was more of an accusation than a question.

"Just showing up for work, Sheriff."

The sheriff and I had become acquainted during the investigation of Martha Tepper's disappearance. I had solved the murder, but it didn't make us fast friends.

I don't think he had quite forgiven me for getting myself shot at. I wasn't too happy about it, either, having been the target, but that didn't seem to matter.

"Well you heard the deputy. Nobody's working here today."

"What happened, Sheriff? I work on the site here, and I know all the guys on the crew. If one of them is hurt, I'd like to know who it is."

Pine Ridge is a small town. The sheriff would know all the regulars on Barry's crew. He should be able to tell me *something.*

"We don't think it's any of the crew, Miss Neverall. None of us recognize him.

"I called Barry, and he'll be here soon. But he's already been notified that you can't proceed until we've finished our investigation into the accident."

He turned and walked away. "Go home,"

he said without turning around.

I went back to the Bug and climbed into the driver's seat, but I couldn't shake the feeling that I needed to stay. I reached for my thermos, grateful that I had been organized enough to make coffee this morning.

That's where Barry found me.

His truck pulled up next to me, and I looked over at the mud-caked tires even with my window. A minute later Barry's face appeared in the window, and I wound down the glass.

"Sheriff Mitchell said he closed down the site and was sending everybody home."

"Not everyone," I said, looking pointedly at Sean's pickup, parked a few yards away. "But he wouldn't talk to *me*."

"Nothing personal, girl, uh, Georgie," he amended quickly. Barry was trying to come into the twenty-first century.

"Sean was the first one here, and he's the one that called the sheriff. That's all."

I shrugged. "Maybe so. But who's hurt? He says he doesn't think it's one of our guys, but who else would be out here at this hour?"

"That's what I'm here to find out." Barry patted the windowsill and straightened.

I didn't wait for an invitation. I jumped out of the car and followed him toward the flashing lights. He didn't try to stop me.

Deputy Wheeler stepped forward to block our path, as he had done earlier, but Sheriff Mitchell spotted Barry and called out to him.

Barry glanced at Wheeler. "Sheriff wants to talk to me," he said as he passed the deputy.

I stuck close to Barry, as though I belonged. This time Wheeler gave me a sour look, but he let me pass.

I wasn't exactly hiding behind Barry, but I figured if Mitchell didn't notice me he couldn't send me back to my car.

We passed through the ring of official vehicles, the red-and-blue lights casting garish shadows across our faces.

Firefighters in heavy turnouts and hard hats stood at the lip of the moat, looking down into it. From below, I could hear muffled voices and the splash of booted feet in the water at the bottom.

As we moved closer there was no sense of urgency in the men, no rush to get the injured man to the ambulance. No one was in any hurry.

Not good.

Sheriff Mitchell led Barry to the edge of the moat and I trailed along behind. The firefighters moved aside, clearing our view of the muddy bottom.

The beams of heavy-duty flashlights cut through the mist in the moat. The reflected light cast crazy shadows, throwing the scene at the bottom into chaos.

My brain struggled to make a recognizable image from the jumble. The moat itself was a place I knew well, and I could sort out the steep sides and the temporary bridge.

But the bottom didn't look right. As I looked harder I saw three paramedics, the reflective tape on their brown jackets spelling out "Clackamas Fire."

The fog shifted and I got a brief clear look at the scene below.

I don't know what I expected to see. But I didn't expect to see a pair of hand-stitched Italian loafers motionless at the bottom of the moat — their owner lying partway under the temporary bridge, his upper body hidden by the piers and planks. But I knew those shoes.

I gasped. Several heads swiveled my direction, and Sheriff Mitchell quirked an eyebrow. "Someone you know, Miss Neverall?"

"No. Yes. I — maybe," I stuttered. "All I can see are the shoes, really, so how can I say?"

The sheriff gave me a hard look. "Don't

go anywhere. As soon as Doc Cox gets here, you can take a look at the rest of him. In the meantime, stay out of the way."

I didn't ask why they were waiting for Dr. Cox. The answer was clear in the lack of urgency. This wasn't a rescue.

The body attached to those shoes was dead.

CHAPTER 7

I told myself it wasn't my fault Blake had managed to drown in the few inches of water, but I still felt guilty. After all, hadn't I just been wishing that he would go away and stay away?

It looked like I got my wish, but it didn't make me happy. I'd wanted him gone, not dead.

Barry called the office and reassigned the crew to other jobs — except for Sean and me. We were at the McComb site until the sheriff let us go.

Barry said Sean had found Blake in the moat. What had Blake been doing out here before the crew arrived? The man I knew wouldn't have been caught dead . . .

Ooh, bad choice of words.

Besides, he'd been here just yesterday.

He had a job. But was that a reason to come out here in the middle of the night?

Dr. Cox slid his way down the side of the

moat to where Blake's body lay, and I watched from above. The sheriff followed him down, and the two men stood at the bottom conferring as the doctor examined the body.

The doctor was only down there a couple minutes before the paramedics signaled to their crew above. A litter was lowered down the slope, and they rolled the body into it.

The irony was not lost on me. Blake Weston — the man who wouldn't go to the dog park with me because he might get something on his shoe — had drowned in the dirty rain water at the bottom of an unfinished moat.

I wondered how he would have explained that to his friends. Would I even know his friends now?

Or at least his family. I seemed to remember a brother in Salinas — or something like that — and a mother in the Bay Area.

The stretcher inched up the side of the trench, but instead of having me look as they brought Blake up, the sheriff pulled me aside behind a truck.

"The doc said he's going to need a little time with this guy, so he asked me to bring you by in a couple hours. Give him a chance to find out what killed him, and clean him up a little before you look at him."

I nodded.

Truthfully, I hadn't been overjoyed at the idea of looking at him at all. At least this would give me some time to . . .

To what? Think about it? To dread the encounter?

Maybe waiting wasn't such a good idea. Maybe I should just get it over with.

But the sheriff already had me by the arm, and was walking quickly toward my car. "I could take you with me," he said, "but that would leave your car stuck up here. Unless you want to have someone come get it?"

Something in his tone made me think that having my own car would be a very good idea.

The offer of a ride? Probably not a chivalrous gesture.

I turned down the hill away from the Mc-Comb site. A last look in the rearview mirror showed a covered litter sliding into the back of the ambulance. It was instantly replaced by the front end of the sheriff's cruiser as he pulled in behind me.

I observed every speed limit all the way to the station, acutely aware of the sheriff a few car lengths behind me.

As I drove, I considered calling someone. But who would I call? None of my friends nor my mother knew anything about my life in San Francisco. A call to any of them would invite questions I wasn't ready to answer.

I tried to remember the names of the people who'd been part of Samurai Security; people who might remember me or Blake, or both of us.

There were several names I would never forget. Their numbers had been in the company cell phone left on the executive desk with my letter of resignation.

And what would I say if I could call them?

Hi. Haven't talked to you in years. By the way, have you seen Blake Weston lately? He just showed up in my hometown, and now he's dead.

Yeah, that would make for interesting conversation.

No. I was on my own.

Sheriff Mitchell kept me waiting for nearly an hour in the lobby of the station. I passed the time sitting in an institutional molded-plastic chair that made my right leg go to sleep and reading months-old copies of police news magazines.

By the time he called me in to his office the initial shock had worn off, I had passed the point of semi-cheerful cooperation, and moved on to annoyed inconvenience. If I couldn't work today, there were a lot of other things I would rather do than hang around the sheriff's office waiting to tell him as little as possible about Blake Weston.

He waved me to a chair and sat down behind his desk.

The vinyl-padded, metal office chair was an improvement over the molded plastic in the waiting room, though not by much. I sat stiffly on the edge of the seat, waiting impatiently.

He kept looking at me, then back down to the file that was open on his desk — neither view improved his mood — and his face was as grim and clouded as the weather.

"Miss Neverall" — he shook his head — "what is it with you and my crime scenes?"

"It's where I work! I was supposed to be there, just like I have been every morning." I was getting tired of defending myself for turning up for work.

Then I realized what else he had said. "And, crime scene? What do you mean? Just because some idiot wanders into a construction site in the dark and manages to fall in a moat and drown?"

"If by 'some idiot' you mean a former associate of yours, and by 'drown' you mean suffer fatal injuries, then that is exactly what I mean."

The second part stopped me, but only for

a second. "Well, falling into the moat in the dark would cause injuries, wouldn't it? I mean, there wasn't any light out there."

I sat back a little. This conversation was not going the way I planned. I waited for the sheriff's reply.

"Let's try this again, Miss Neverall. It appears you knew the deceased." He looked at the file again. "Blake Weston, with an address on Bush Street in San Francisco." He looked back up at me. "You knew Mr. Weston?"

I nodded. "Several years ago. We were business associates." The rest of it had nothing to do with Blake's accident. No need to go into ancient history.

"And Mr. Weston had made multiple visits to the job site?"

I nodded again.

The sheriff waited, but I didn't add anything.

"And there was an encounter yesterday morning? Mr. Weston was" — he glanced at his notes — " 'hassling' you?"

I hoped the surprise I felt wasn't evident on my face. Blake had been a jerk, but I'd lost my temper and yelled at him in front of the crew. Someone was evidently looking out for me.

"There was an encounter, as you call it.

Mr. Weston came to the site. He was rude. I know you aren't supposed to speak ill of the dead, but rude was pretty standard for him. His behavior yesterday didn't seem much different from the last time I saw him."

Understatement, much?

I glanced at the folder on the desk, but the sheriff kept it tilted enough that I couldn't see what was in it. "You are sure it was Blake Weston?" I asked. "I mean, all I saw were his shoes, really."

"It was Weston. There was a California license in his wallet."

"So what makes this a crime scene? He wandered out there in the dark and fell in the moat." I leaned forward. "I know that sounds pretty stupid, but you have to remember that Blake is — was — a city guy. It wouldn't really occur to him how dark it would be out there."

The sheriff gave me a sharp look. "How do you know so much about a business associate, Miss Neverall?"

Whoa. Maybe I was being a little too helpful.

"We worked together in San Francisco, and it was obvious to *everybody* that Blake was a city guy. The closest he came to outdoor activities was an occasional sidewalk café."

70

The sheriff nodded and scribbled something in his file and closed it. He folded his hands on top of it.

"That's all for now, Miss Neverall. I don't think we will need you to identify the body, after all." He glanced at the closed file. "It's not something you want to see anyway."

I took the hint and let myself out.

It wasn't until I was driving home that I realized he had never actually answered my questions.

Why was the moat considered a crime scene?

Was the death of Blake Weston really an accident?

CHAPTER 8

When I pulled into the driveway, I was greeted by frantic barking from inside the house. Daisy and Buddha knew the sound of the Volkswagen's old four-banger, and they knew it meant a trip to the backyard.

On my way through the kitchen to the back door, I glanced at the answering machine. The light was blinking. No surprise there. News traveled fast in a small town. Everyone I know probably called to find out what happened.

I wished I had an answer.

But before I could listen to the calls, there was a knock at the front door.

"Georgie?"

It was Wade.

His expression was a mixture of concern and exasperation when I opened the door.

"Are you okay?" he asked, coming in without an invitation and putting his arm around me.

"I heard you were at the sheriff's office for questioning about the body they found this morning. But by the time I got there you had already left.

"I got here as quick as I could."

I gave Wade a quick hug. His concern was sweet, but the gossip machine had obviously been working overtime.

"The guys are out back," I said, leading him back through the kitchen to check on the dogs.

They were exploring the backyard as though it was someplace new and exotic, even though they had been out there only a few hours earlier. It made me smile.

I turned back to Wade. "I'm glad you came to check on me, but it really isn't a big deal. The sheriff heard I knew the guy, and he wanted to ask me about him."

"You knew the guy?" Wade reached out and took my hand. "Are you sure you're okay?"

"Sure," I said brightly, as though I was accustomed to ghosts rising up out of my past and then dropping dead. "It's not like we were best friends or anything," I lied.

Guilt rolled over me. Lying was becoming a habit since Blake Weston had reappeared. It was the only way I could keep my secrets, but that didn't mean I had to like it.

"Seriously?" Wade looked in my eyes, and I forced myself to hold his gaze, mentally begging him to accept my story.

He finally nodded, and squeezed my hand. "If you say so," he said.

I could see the political scales tilting in his brain. How to cope with the latest scandal by association? Months earlier I had helped solve the disappearance of Martha Tepper, and Wade had to work out a balancing act.

Daisy and Buddha appeared at the back door, whining for their treats.

Wade released my hand and the moment passed. I knew he had reservations about my story, but he trusted me not to mess up his life.

I hoped his trust wasn't misplaced.

"Was this that guy Gregory was harassing you about at dinner?" Wade asked.

"You thought he was harassing me?" Apparently Wade hadn't missed the antagonism in Gregory's questions.

"Well, badgering, at the very least. He seemed to think he was entitled to some information or explanation, or something."

"Yeah. Well. Not that I owe him anything. No matter what his thing is with my mother."

Wade arched an eyebrow at me. Everybody seemed able to do that but me and it was annoying. "You're actually referring to his relationship with the inimitable Sandra?"

"Not in specifics!" I warned. "Just that they're a couple, and he thinks it gives him special status with me. Not likely."

Even though I was a grown woman and my mother had been a widow for more than four years, her romantic entanglements made me uncomfortable. She was dating Gregory. Beyond that I chose not to go.

Wade took the hint. "So what was it he thought you should tell him? I mean, if this guy is dead, maybe you should talk about him."

I shook my head. "We were business associates. I didn't like him much." That was an understatement. By the time I left the city, I loathed the man.

"And?"

"And I hadn't seen him in years until he showed up out at the job site." I scowled. "Which I have said about a thousand times in the last couple days. Can we just let it go?"

My stomach grumbled, reminding me all I'd consumed all day was a thermos full of black coffee. I glanced at the clock, amazed to see that it was already past lunch hour.

I offered Wade a sandwich while I frantically tried to remember if I had anything to make a sandwich *with*. He declined and said he had to get back to the office, if I was sure I was okay.

I thought about the blinking light on the answering machine, and the calls I would have to return once he left. It was tempting to ask him to stay, but he did have an accounting practice to run and I had already taken him away from the office when he should be working.

Besides, he likely would keep bringing up the subject of Blake Weston and I didn't want to talk about him. Ever.

"No," I said. The regret in my voice was genuine. I really did wish he could stay, if only so I could postpone those phone messages. "I appreciate the offer, but you need to get back to the office, and I have stuff I should do."

By the time Wade's car pulled away I was already regretting my decision. I could use the distraction. The realization was sinking in. Blake Weston, a man I had once known well, was dead.

And he was dead in a way that made no sense.

When I thought about Blake's death — and I didn't seem capable of thinking of anything else — there were lots of questions, but no answers.

What was Blake doing in Pine Ridge? He had steadfastly refused to leave the city for any reason in all the time I had known him.

Why was he palling around with Chad McComb? I was sure they didn't know each other, yet Blake had acted all buddy-buddy with Chad and Astrid.

For that matter, what was Samurai Security doing on this job to begin with? I mean, it was a job I'd have taken in a heartbeat, but it certainly didn't fit with the "new direction" the board had cited when they'd tossed me out of my own company.

Why was Blake out at the job site in the dark? There was nothing there for him to see particularly, and he wasn't fond of the outdoors.

Another thing that didn't make sense was how he died. Sure, babies could drown in a few inches of water, but they were small and helpless. Blake was a full-grown man, perfectly capable of getting himself out of the water.

Unless he hit his head on the way down, or fainted, or something.

None of it made any sense.

My stomach growled loudly, reminding me a thermos of black coffee met only my daily caffeine requirements. There were several other food groups — sugar, salt, chocolate — and I should eat something.

I opened my refrigerator and stared at the contents — half a loaf of bread, not too stale; a couple eggs; a slice of pizza of indeterminate age; condiment packages from the drive-through; and a nearly empty jar of marmalade.

It was a bachelor fridge, a bad habit acquired in my high-tech life of hundred-hour workweeks and twenty-four-hour takeout. My mother would be appalled.

I stared into the fridge as though that would make something edible magically appear, but it wasn't working.

The phone rang, and I ignored it.

I kept staring at the empty refrigerator, but instead of seeing stale bread I kept picturing Blake's hand-stitched Italian loafers toes down in the water at the bottom of the moat.

CHAPTER 9

The answering machine picked up, and I listened to myself telling the caller I wasn't home. The message finished, and I heard Sue's voice.

"Georgie? Are you there, Georgie? Pick up, girl!! I heard there was an accident out at the McComb job site. Paula called me, said some guy was hurt or something, but she wouldn't really know anything until Barry gets home."

Paula Ciccone, the town librarian, was Barry's wife. He must have called her while we were at the sheriff's station, and she called Sue. News traveled fast in Pine Ridge.

Paula was much more than my boss's wife. The investigation of Martha Tepper's disappearance and murder had drawn her into Sue's and my friendship, and made us a threesome.

Sue paused, waiting for me to answer. After a few seconds she continued, "I'm at work, you know the number. Just call me, please. I need to know you're okay!"

I gave up on the refrigerator.

Maybe I could just drive through some-place, or pick up some takeout from the deli in the grocery store. But if I wanted to eat I was going to have to leave the house. And no matter where I went in Pine Ridge, *somebody* would want to ask me about what happened at the job site.

Another thought struck me like a bucket of cold water.

With Blake dead, it was likely someone else from Samurai would take his place. There was every possibility that some other ghost from my past would show up at any minute.

Buddha bumped up against my leg. He stuck his head under my hand, begging to be petted. He didn't do that often, and only when I was upset. Clearly, he sensed my agitation.

I sighed and rubbed his ears. There was no way I could keep what happened in San Francisco a secret for much longer. I had to trust someone.

I walked to the front door and pulled the leashes from the hook. "Come on guys," I called. "Let's go to the spa."

■ ■ ■ ■

Sue just nodded when I came through the front door of Doggy Day Spa with Daisy and Buddha on their leashes. It was like she'd been expecting me.

She had a beagle on the grooming table, clipping his nails.

"About time you showed up, Neverall."

"I'm hungry," I said lamely. "You want to get some lunch?"

Sue glanced at Daisy and Buddha. "You know someplace that will serve Airedales?"

I chuckled. "Figured they'd stay here and guard the place, and maybe I could get you to give them a bath after we eat."

Sue finished with the beagle, and lifted him off the table. She put him in one of the kennels in the back of the shop and slipped him a green treat, all the while crooning to him in baby talk.

After the beagle was tucked away with a scratch behind the ears, she walked back up front and skimmed the appointment book. "Colleen will be here to pick up Peanut in a few minutes and we can go. The afternoon's pretty quiet, so I should have time for the guys."

Sue snapped her fingers. "In fact, I could

use your help." She dug around on the desk for a minute and came up with one of the thumb drives I'd insisted she get. We traded grooming for computer services, and it looked like it was time for me to pay up.

"I can't get the computer to read this thing. I plug it in and nothing happens."

She handed me the drive. "Where do you want to have lunch?" It was another one of Sue's conversational U-turns.

I checked my watch. "Dee's?" Dee's Lunch was close and cheap, and it would be near closing time. With luck, the place would be empty.

"Works for me. You want to take a look at the computer?"

The bell over the front door rang, interrupting our conversation. Colleen came in and claimed Peanut. She stuffed some bills in Sue's hand, and hurried out without asking me about the accident. I took that as a good sign.

We put the dogs in the big pen at the back of the shop, locked up, and walked down Main Street toward Dee's Lunch. It was just down the block, past the Radio Shack franchise and across the street from Katie's Bakery.

The aroma of fresh bread wafted across from Katie's and I knew I'd have to take a loaf home with me. The stuff in the refrigerator was past its prime anyway.

Dee's was barely wide enough to hold a lunch counter along one wall and a handful of tiny two-seat booths along the other. The kitchen was a gas grill, a couple deep fryers, and a decidedly low-tech coffeemaker. She refused to consider an espresso machine, and her one concession to the twenty-first century was a minuscule microwave oven, which was only used to heat pie.

Dee herself seemed as ancient as the coffeemaker. She had served breakfast and lunch as far back as I could remember, and she locked the front door promptly at 2:00 P.M. every day. If you showed up hungry at 2:01, you were out of luck.

Fortunately for us, it was only one thirty, and Dee was behind the counter, topping up the coffee cups of a couple bank tellers on a late lunch hour.

Sue and I walked past the three empty booths and slid into the last one in the back. I took the side facing the door, where I could see if anyone else came in.

Dee looked up and smiled a welcome. She didn't bother with menus, since the selection never changed. Instead, she set two glasses of iced tea on the counter, waved at Sue, and busied herself at the grill.

Sue retrieved the iced tea and set the frosty glasses on the table. It was cold and gloomy outside but the diner was nearly twenty degrees warmer — thanks to the grill and the fryers — and the cool beverage was welcome.

Besides, I wasn't sure I trusted the coffee. I was pretty sure that pot was older than me.

We sipped at the tea, Sue watching me over the rim of her glass. Finally, she set the glass down. "Well?"

"Well what? Can't I get hungry?"

"Yeah. And you'd go visit Mayor Mc-Cheese. Or get Garibaldi's to deliver. You wouldn't come down here without calling, with the lame excuse that you wanted to get the dogs bathed." She stopped for breath, then added, "Especially that part about the dogs. You're usually very good about checking my appointments first."

"Thank you for recognizing that," I replied lightly. "I am nothing if not kind and considerate."

Sue snorted. "You know what I mean, Neverall. There's something on your mind, and you're stalling."

Sue was right. I had made up my mind to trust someone — to trust her — but now that I was here it was hard to know where

84

to start. How much did I have to tell her?

My life in San Francisco had been a taboo subject for a long time. I told myself I didn't want anyone to know about the humiliation and failure, but now I did want to get at least some of it off my chest. While I was trying to figure out what — and how much — to say, Dee came hobbling out from behind the counter, two heavy white plates in her gnarled hands. She refused to surrender to the arthritis. She said working at the Lunch was what kept her going and she wouldn't know what to do with her time if she quit.

She set a patty melt and fries in front of Sue, and a club sandwich with onion rings in front of me. It was the same thing we'd eaten every visit since we were in high school. There was something reassuring about a place where they knew what you wanted without asking.

I suspected what Dee would really miss if she retired was the chance to be in the middle of everything that went on in town. If Tiny's was the local gathering place in the evening and on the weekends, Dee's was the only place to get a decent breakfast or a quick lunch. It was usually busy from the first coffee at 6 A.M. to the last burger at 2. Everybody ate at Dee's.

Including, I realized too late, Sandra and Gregory. Who were walking through the front door.

I must have looked as trapped as I felt. Sue's eyes widened, and she whirled around quickly to see what had caused my reaction.

She turned back and shrugged. "Looks like we have some company."

I grimaced.

Sandra spotted me, and dropped Gregory's hand. She walked back to where Sue and I sat and gave my shoulder a quick squeeze. "I heard there was an accident, Georgiana. Are you okay? You weren't hurt, were you?"

"No, Mother." I looked up and saw real concern in her face. No matter how little we understood each other, I was still her only child.

I reached up and squeezed her hand. "I'm okay. Really."

She looked at Gregory who waited at the counter, radiating impatience. "We're just picking up sandwiches to take back to the office," she explained, turning back to me. "Are you sure you're okay?"

I nodded and smiled. "Sure, Mom." I hoped she would be reassured.

She looked from me to Gregory and back again. Dee was already putting food in a brown paper bag, and it was clear Gregory was in a hurry.

"Go on, Mom. Your food's ready."

My mother hesitated, her expression troubled.

"Really, Mom. I'm fine."

"You will call me, Georgiana? Soon?"

I crossed my fingers under the table, like I'd done when I was eight years old. "Sure."

Sue watched me closely, as if she could see through the table to my crossed fingers.

Mom gave me one last look. "Call me," she repeated as she turned back toward the front door.

Gregory tossed some bills on the counter and followed my mother out the door without looking back.

"You won't call."

"I had my fingers crossed," I protested.

"Georgie! What are you, ten?" Sue rolled her eyes. "You shouldn't lie to your mother."

"I wasn't lying, exactly. I will call her. Eventually."

I bit into my sandwich. The toast crunched and I tasted salty bacon. It tasted exactly the way it had when I was a teenager. The ripe tomato dripped juice and seeds onto the plate. I wondered where Dee got tomatoes this good.

Sue dunked the corner of her patty melt

in the pool of ketchup on her plate, and took a bite. I could smell the grilled onions that oozed out the sides of her sandwich.

"I know that. No, I meant the other lie," she said around a mouthful of beef and rye toast. "The one about being fine."

Once again, Sue's conversation had swooped around and landed exactly where I didn't want it to go.

No, that wasn't true. I was here because I did want to go there. I wanted to tell someone about Blake. I wanted to let Sue in to a little corner of my old life.

Maybe.

"Okay, I'm not fine. Not entirely."

Sue stopped, a French fry halfway to her mouth.

"Did I hear that right? The original tough girl admitting she isn't okay?"

I nodded. "This situation actually has me kind of spooked."

Sue washed the fry down with a gulp of tea. Her voice turned serious. "Georgie, nothing spooks you. Ever. You nearly got caught breaking into Martha Tepper's house, you got shot at and ended up in the hospital and you just shrugged it off. Now some stranger gets hurt on a construction site, and you're spooked?"

I picked up an onion ring and broke it

88

into little pieces, building a mound of golden breading in the middle of my plate, hemmed in by the remaining pieces of sandwich. It was pretty much how I felt.

"He's dead, Sue." I looked up at her shocked face, and hurried on. "Looks like he drowned in the moat — is that a stupid way to go, or what? — and Sean found him there when he got to the site this morning."

"Okay," she said slowly. "That's creepy. Is that what's bothering you, that he died in the place you were working?"

"Yeah." I pushed the food around on my plate. My appetite had disappeared. Sue reached over and snagged a ring without asking — another thing that hadn't changed since high school.

"Thanks," she said, waving the ring. "But it sounds like there's more. Is there?"

Dee hobbled over and refilled our tea. She dropped the separate checks — like always — on the table. She walked to the front and turned the "Open" sign over, then went back behind the counter and turned off the grill.

I glanced at my wrist. I was still wearing the battered plastic watch I wore for work, and it said two o'clock, straight up. I looked at Sue.

"Gotta go."

We each grabbed a check and dug in our pockets for cash. Dee didn't like to mess with plastic, a fact the occasional tourist had to learn the hard way. Locals knew to carry cash if they wanted lunch at Dee's.

We carried our plates to the counter, as though we were back in the high school cafeteria. Somehow, it had always seemed like the right thing to do.

I started to cross to Katie's when we walked out, but Sue grabbed my arm and pulled me toward her shop.

"You were telling me about the accident," she said, "and there was something more you were going to say. You can get your bread fix later."

Daisy and Buddha greeted us with happy barks when we unlocked the shop. They knew Sue was a soft touch and she didn't disappoint them, slipping them each a green treat.

She didn't get them ready for a bath, though. Instead, she sat down on her stool behind the counter and motioned me to the other stool.

"Now, make like Paul Harvey," she said. "I want the rest of the story."

"I knew the guy."

"But you said it wasn't anyone on the crew, Georgie. And if it wasn't anyone from

Pine Ridge, who was it?"

"Someone I used to work with."

"The guy from Tiny's?" she exclaimed. "The hunk with the designer wardrobe and the four-hundred-dollar haircut?"

My brain, the part that didn't want to deal with Blake's death, wondered how Sue knew about four-hundred-dollar haircuts, much less had the ability to spot one.

"That's the guy that fell in the moat?"

"His name is — was — Blake Weston." I crossed my arms over my stomach, as if I could hold myself together that way. "We were friends, then more than friends. It ended badly, and I hadn't seen him in several years."

"Until he walked into Tiny's." Sue finished my thought. "No wonder you looked like you'd seen a ghost. He didn't seem much like your type, though. Way too slick."

I chuckled. "And what is my type?"

Sue reddened. "You know what I mean, Georgie. You're a plumber now, and you hang around with people like me and Paula and Wade — and none of us exactly have a designer wardrobe, unless you include Wrangler and Fruit of the Loom on the list."

"I'm still an apprentice," I reminded her. "And I hang out with people like you because you and Paula and Wade are my friends. But that doesn't mean I didn't have other kinds of friends before I came back to Pine Ridge."

"Did you?" Sue said. "Have other kinds of friends?"

Unfolding my arms, I stood up and walked across the shop. My back was to Sue. "I don't know."

I fiddled with a display of cat toys, lining them up carefully on their metal peg. "I knew a lot of people in San Francisco, and I worked and socialized with them. But I don't know if they were friends."

The gloom was getting to me. I squared my shoulders and turned to face Sue. I steadied my voice and forced a matter-of-fact tone as I summarized my years at Samurai.

"After I got my master's degree, I started a computer security company. When I started expanding, Blake was my first partner, and we did well. The computer industry was exploding, and we were the hot new thing.

"Guys with money came looking for us, offering to help us grow. They didn't want to interfere in how we ran the company, or so they said. But when the industry started cooling off, they changed their minds.

"I knew a lot of things about hardware

and software" — I walked back to the counter, and picked up the thumb drive we'd left sitting there before lunch — "but not a lot about office politics. Blake did.

"When the money guys decided to 'go in a different direction' " — I made air quotes with my fingers — "I was the one who left." I forced a smile I didn't feel, and hoped it wasn't too obvious. "And now you know, the rest of the story." I mimicked the popular radio host's signature line.

Sue glanced at the thumb drive I held loosely in my hand. "That's how you know all that stuff about cookies and worms and spyware and all that stuff you told me about? That was the kind of stuff you were doing?"

"Among other things." I shrugged. "But I left all that down there, and I don't want to do it anymore." I grinned again, and this time I did feel it. "You and Barry are the only ones I make an exception for."

"So this Blake guy was, what? More than somebody you worked with, that's for sure. Are we talking close business partner, or maybe ex-boyfriend?"

"We dated," I hedged. That wasn't a lie, exactly. It had been a little more serious than that, at least on my part, but a girl has to have some pride. I wasn't ready to admit he'd been willing to dump me the instant the investors offered him the corner office.

"And Sandra doesn't know any of this, does she?"

I shook my head. "Would you tell her?"

Sue burst into giggles. "No way!"

I tossed the thumb drive up and caught it. "Now, let me see if I can figure out what's wrong with this thing."

I walked back into the office, feeling better than I had since the day I spotted Blake at the McComb job site. I was sad he was dead — we had been close once — but I could stop thinking about him for a little while.

A very little while.

CHAPTER 10

I arrived home with a better attitude, freshly groomed dogs, and a feeling of accomplishment. The thumb drive problem had turned out to be a simple conflict caused by connecting two drives at the same time. All I had to do was disconnect the other drive, and everything was fine.

I thought about what might have caused the problem as I fed the dogs and checked the refrigerator for dinner.

Same stuff that was there at lunchtime, plus a fresh loaf of whole wheat from Katie's sitting on the counter. I'd stopped in after I'd solved Sue's computer issue.

The stale bread gave me an idea. A quick check of the cupboard turned up cinnamon and vanilla. With eggs and stale bread I had French toast, and the dregs of the marmalade would substitute for syrup.

My mother would be proud.

The pan was hot, and I had just put the

first bread slices in when my cell phone rang. I didn't recognize the number, but the area code was familiar.

San Francisco.

Another ghost.

I let the phone play its cheery ringtone. I knew the call would ruin my mood, and my evening. I could just let it go to voice mail, and worry about it later. Or tomorrow. Or next week.

But if I did that there was a good chance that the ghost, whoever he was, would show up in Pine Ridge. Ignoring the call wouldn't make a difference. Besides, I'd obsess about it the rest of the evening if I didn't pick up.

"Hello."

"Is this Georgiana Neverall?" The voice was vaguely familiar. I had heard it before, but it was older and deeper than I remembered.

"Speaking."

"Georgie! It's so good to hear your voice. How are you?" This time, the voice squeaked a little at the end, and a face attached itself to the memory.

Richard Parks. He was an intern at Samurai, a student from the local community college with too little money and a terrifying talent. I swore the boy dreamed in machine code, the way fluent foreign language students dreamed in French or German. Within his first week I had realized he could have my job if he wanted it.

I wondered if he did.

"Richard?" I asked.

"Yeah, Georgie, it's me! It's really good to talk to you again. I mean, the circumstances and all, that's not so cool, in fact it's really terrible. But I just never thought we'd hear from you, after you took that buyout and moved away. And then Blake called and said he'd run into you in some tiny town up in Oregon, but he hadn't got a chance to talk to you."

Richard's words rushed out, piling on top of one another, and threatened to overwhelm me. It took a few seconds for the meaning to sink in.

"Buyout?"

"Oh! I'm not supposed to know about that, am I? Forget I said it, okay? It was just that everybody knew, and it's been a long time, and . . ." His voice trailed off.

"What are you talking about, Richard? And how did you get my cell number anyway?"

"From the sheriff. He called here about Blake, and I might have mentioned that I knew you and did he know how I could get in touch with you, since I knew you were up there." I could picture Richard's baby face — heck, he *was* a baby — with a blush creeping up his neck. Richard may have been a computer genius, but he was still just an awkward kid.

"Blake told you he ran into me?" I was still trying to process the torrent of words.

"He said he bumped into you in a local restaurant. Told Stan Fischer he didn't get much chance to talk, but he figured he'd see you later and catch up. That's all I heard, but I know Stan talked to him a couple times."

I remembered Stan Fischer all too well — the eight-hundred-pound gorilla of the investors, and one of the architects of my ouster. The legend was he'd made his money working the Alaska pipeline in the seventies, and come back to California to invest it. He'd done well, but money and age hadn't smoothed out any of the rough edges. He'd gone through several wives, a couple girlfriends, and there was office gossip about Stan and an intern. He still looked and acted like a roughneck.

"So Stan's running things now?"

"Well, Blake's in charge, but Stan's pretty involved. That is," he amended hastily, "Blake *was* in charge. I guess Stan's taking care of things for now. You know, until we can figure things out."

"So, Richard, about that buyout? What was it you heard?"

"Nothing. Nothing at all, Georgie. I didn't say a thing, okay?" He sounded more than embarrassed. He sounded scared.

"It's not a big deal, Richard. I just wondered what people had heard."

"What I heard was that there was a confidentiality agreement, and if anyone talked about it they'd be fired. You know this industry, Georgie. If somebody got canned here, they'd have a tough time finding another good job."

I nodded, without realizing Richard couldn't see me. Of course. He was afraid of losing his job if he talked about my nonexistent buyout.

I caught a whiff of something burning.

My dinner!

"Frack!" I dropped the phone on the table, and grabbed the frying pan. The toast in the pan was turning black around the edges. I dumped the whole mess into the sink, and turned off the stove.

I'd deal with it later.

"Georgiana?" Richard's voice was tiny, carrying from where I'd abandoned the phone. "Georgie? Are you still there?"

I grabbed the phone back up. "Sorry,

Richard. I was trying to burn dinner." I glanced at the blackened mess in the sink. "Looks like I did a pretty good job, too."

"I'm sorry. I called at a bad time. Maybe I should just call you back later, or something."

"Never mind, Richard. It's fine." I thought for a second. "But just why did you call me? It's been a long time since I left Samurai, after all."

"Actually, it's about Stan. He's at the San Francisco airport, and he's catching the next flight to Portland. He should be up there in a couple hours, and he said he'd like to talk to you while he's there."

"Ooookay," I said slowly. "I don't know why he'd want to talk to me, but you can pass along my number."

"I don't know, either, Georgie. I just know he asked me to find you and let him know how to get in touch." Richard hesitated, and I could picture him, his mouth twisted as he pondered his next words. "You won't tell him what I said, will you, Georgie? I mean, I know I wasn't supposed to know and all, but it just slipped out. I swear, I won't talk to anybody else about it or anything. I won't even tell them I talked to you if you don't want me to. Except for Stan, of course."

"Sure, Richard. There isn't any reason for

me to mention it to Stan. I'm not even sure I'll actually talk to him, since there isn't anything I can really tell him."

I finally got Richard off the phone, and turned back to inspect the wreckage of my dinner. The French toast was burned, I was out of eggs, and the frying pan was a crusted mess.

I called Garibaldi's and ordered a pizza.

My mother didn't have to know.

While I waited for the delivery driver, I thought about what Richard had said. "Everybody" at Samurai knew I'd taken a buyout? They thought I'd walked away with a bundle of cash and left them all behind.

No wonder no one had called. And I just bet that rumor was strategically "leaked" to the entire company as soon as I was out the door. It certainly would have sounded better than the truth — that Blake and the board of directors that included Stan Fischer had cheated me out of the company, and left me without a dime.

And Stan was on his way to Pine Ridge. I wanted to see him even less than I wanted to see Blake. The last time I'd seen him was when I left San Francisco with my tail between my legs. It would be awkward; more so because Stan didn't have the social grace and charm of Blake Weston.

Okay, so the charm had worn a bit thin, judging by the way Blake had talked to me out at the job site, but he had been charming when he wanted to be.

The doorbell rang, and I grabbed my wallet. In spite of everything that was going on, I was still hungry.

But it wasn't the pizza delivery guy. It was Sheriff Mitchell.

And he didn't look happy.

CHAPTER 11

"Good evening, Miss Neverall. May I come in?"

The tone of his voice didn't give me much hope that a protest would do any good. It had that we-can-do-this-the-easy-way-or-the-hard-way quality you hear in all the cop shows on TV.

It had the desired effect. I opened the door wide and invited him in.

I glanced outside as I closed the door behind the sheriff. His cruiser was parked at the curb, but he appeared to be alone. It looked like an official visit, but at least there weren't lights and sirens.

"Have a seat, Sheriff." I waved at the sofa, but he remained standing. "I was waiting for a delivery from Garibaldi's. In fact" — I held out the wallet as proof — "that's who I thought was at the door."

I smiled at him. "Seems like the last time you were here Garibaldi's was delivering, too. If I recall, you like extra olives and pepperoni."

Maybe I shouldn't have reminded him. The last time he'd been in my living room, I'd been recovering from a run-in with the Gladstones who'd killed Martha Tepper and hidden her body.

He gave me an unhappy look, and sat down on the recliner. He didn't lean back but sat up straight, his elbows resting on his knees.

The doorbell rang again. This time it was Garibaldi's. By the time I got back to the living room with the pizza and some napkins, Sheriff Mitchell had a notebook out and he was fiddling with his pen.

"Help yourself," I said, setting the box on the steamer trunk that served as a coffee table. "I always order a large, even though it's way too much."

I was chattering. I knew it and I hated the fact, but my nerves were pulled tight by Richard's phone call and the impending arrival of Stan Fischer. The sheriff's unexpected visit didn't exactly help matters.

"Thanks," the sheriff said. "Maybe later. But for now, I need to ask you a few questions. I thought you might prefer to talk here, rather than down at the station."

Yow. That sounded like a warning.

"I appreciate that. As long as you don't mind if I eat while we talk. It's been kind of a long day, and I'm hungry."

As if to prove my point, I picked up the slice on my plate and took a big bite. The cheese was still hot, burning my tongue as I tried to chew.

I set the plate down, careful not to put it where the dogs could reach. They knew better, but the aroma of pepperoni and cheese was sometimes too much for their obedience training to overcome.

"So," I said, folding my hands together in my lap. "Questions."

The sheriff glanced at his pad and back up at me. "Do you mind if I use the recorder? You know I feel more secure knowing I got the exact response."

He'd done the same thing when he interviewed me about Martha Tepper. I nodded. I'd expected it.

He reached in his pocket and set the tiny machine on the table next to the pizza box.

"That official, huh?" I asked.

"Just a few details, Miss Neverall. I want to be sure I get everything straight. That's all."

I didn't believe him, but I was smart enough not to say so.

He punched a button, tested the recording and played it back, then noted the time and place before he asked his first question.

"You knew the deceased, Blake Weston?"

I nodded. The sheriff rolled his eyes. I had to actually talk for the recorder. "Yes, I knew him."

"When and where did you see him last?"

"You mean before he came to Pine Ridge?"

"Yes. And after."

"Well, let me see. I saw him at the construction site twice, and once in Tiny's. He was at the site on Tuesday morning with Chad McComb, and with Chad and Astrid in Tiny's that night. And then I saw him at the site the next morning."

"And before that?"

"It was several years ago, in San Francisco. As I told you, we worked together. The last time I saw him was when I left the company where we worked."

"That was" — he checked his notebook — "Samurai Security? Where he was still employed?"

"It was Samurai, yes. But I didn't know that he was still employed there." I'm not a very good liar, but I hadn't *known* Blake was still a part of the company until Richard called. It was a fine distinction, but it worked for me. "I had the impression he was still doing the same kind of work, though he didn't say where he was working."

"According to Chad McComb, it was Samurai Security. Said he'd never done business with them before, but they came highly recommended."

He glanced back at his notes. "You hadn't seen Mr. Weston since you left San Francisco?"

"Yes."

"Had you talked to him?"

I glanced at the recorder. The light blinked steadily, my words saved for anyone to hear. "Can we turn that off for a minute?"

The sheriff hesitated, then reached down and killed the power to the recorder. "Why?"

I toyed with a piece of pepperoni. It was greasy, and I wiped my hands on a paper towel.

"Miss Neverall?"

I looked up and caught the sheriff's gaze. I held his eyes for a minute before I looked back down at my plate. "There are several things about my relationship with Mr. Weston that I would prefer to keep private. Once they are on that thing" — I waved at the recorder — "anybody can listen to what I say."

"It's kept secure, Georgie."

I looked up again, startled by his use of my first name. He flashed a sheepish grin. "Let's start over, shall we?"

I nodded and waited for him to continue.

"Georgie, I have heard some things that make me think you know more about Blake Weston than you've been telling me. I need to know what those things are." He held up a hand to stop the question that was already forming on my lips.

"I have my reasons, just like you have yours for not telling me. I can't divulge why I need to know, but I do. So why don't we have some pizza, and talk about good ol' Blake?"

He reached for a piece of pizza. "And you're the one who told me to call you Georgie."

Fred Mitchell knew I had been holding out on him.

I put another slice on my plate and leaned back. "Okay, we can play it that way. But I want you to promise me this doesn't go any further. It's ancient history, and I don't want to be reading about it on the front page of the *Pine Ridge Times*."

"Scout's honor." He held up three fingers in a salute. "Unless it's evidence of a crime, I'll respect your confidence."

"Blake and I had a, um, complicated

relationship. I started the company, it took off, and Blake was the first partner when I expanded. We had a personal relationship in addition to the business partnership."

"That trick never works."

"I know. But I believed we were different."

He gave a harsh laugh. "Doesn't everyone?"

"Yeah. Well." I chewed a bite of pizza, then continued. "We attracted venture capital, like a lot of high-tech companies did at the time. Eventually, the investors decided they wanted a say in how things were done.

"It did not end well."

The sheriff shrugged and took another piece of pizza. "Seems like things were going okay for Weston. Until recently, of course."

It was my turn to shrug. "Really don't know. Like I said, I haven't talked to him since I left San Francisco."

"We all have those kind of stories. Why is it so important to you to keep this a secret?" His expression was genuinely puzzled.

I could have told him about my mother's disapproval and my father's expectations. I could have explained how I was the local girl that made good at the prestigious university. I could talk about pride and self-respect and all the things that made me keep my failures to myself.

"When a girl gets dumped, Sheriff, she doesn't want to tell the whole world."

Although not the most complete response I could have given, it was an explanation he would understand. An explanation that left intact what little dignity I had left.

"About the only thing that's evidence of," I continued, "is embarrassment. And that isn't a crime, is it?"

"If it was," he answered, "I'd need a lot bigger jail."

He levered himself out of the chair and stretched to his full six feet — an imposing sight. Easy to see why Sue was developing a crush on him — even if she wouldn't admit it. I wondered if it was mutual, and how long it would take one or the other of them to act on it.

"I suppose that's all I have for now, Georgie. There may be more questions later, after we know a little more. But for now, I appreciate your candor." He waved at the box on the trunk. "And the pizza."

I stood up and walked him to the door. As he drove away, I considered his last words. After they knew a little more? Blake had fallen in the moat and drowned. There wasn't much to know.

Except what he was doing out there in the first place.

The good news was that maybe Stan Fischer could answer that question.

The bad news was that meant talking to Stan Fischer, a man not noted for his discretion and civility.

I was so dead.

CHAPTER 12

Sleep was out of the question, at least in part because it was only nine o'clock.

I considered calling Sue and telling her about the sheriff's visit. She was definitely a night person, often watching TV or reading until well past midnight, so it was still plenty early to call her.

Except there are some things you never outgrow. And one of those things was my mother's insistence that you never called anyone after 8:00 P.M., unless it was an absolute emergency.

I didn't think Sheriff Mitchell's visit qualified as an emergency. At least I hoped it didn't.

Instead, I changed into my workout clothes. The second bedroom of my little rental was outfitted with mats for martial arts practice. It wasn't as good as sparring and tumbling with a partner, but it still allowed me to practice.

I moved through my routine. The twisting, tumbling, and reaching were far different from the moves I used on the job, and I could feel different muscles stretching and pulling as I worked.

It would be great to have a partner. I had tried to interest Sue but she said she already had a proven method of self-defense. It was called running away. She said it was clear I needed it, though, since I was the one who got shot at and chased by murderers.

I explained to her that martial arts were more about balance and serenity than fighting. She said if she was any more serene, she'd be in a coma.

I didn't have an answer for that one, because she was right. Sue maintained a calm and sunny outlook on life, and seemed quite content. I was the one who needed serenity.

Especially now. Stan Fischer was on his way to Pine Ridge.

In the morning I was no more serene.

I was barely out of bed when the phone rang for the first time. It was Barry.

"The sheriff still has the McComb site under wraps," he said, when I answered. "We can't work out there until he's through, and I don't have anything else going today."

"That's okay, Bear." It was a nickname I didn't use often, though it fit him. He was my boss, after all, even though he sometimes felt like the older brother I'd never had. "There's some work at the Homes for Hope house that's been waiting for me to have some spare time. I can catch up on a couple projects over there today."

"You sure? I might be able to get you a couple hours in the office."

"I don't think Angie would appreciate my help," I said. "She has things running just fine without me messing it up."

"Well, if you're sure." Barry sounded relieved. There was no need for anyone else in the office, but he knew I needed the money.

"I'm fine, Barry. Got the month covered."

"That's good then. By the way, Paula says to stop by and have some coffee if you're downtown. Says she hasn't seen you in a while."

"Tell her I will. The Hope house should only be a couple hours of work, unless they find something else for me to do. I'll swing by after I'm through."

It was a luxury to have some extra time in the morning. I let the dogs out and made a pot of coffee.

The Hope house crew didn't start as early

114

as Barry did, so I even had time for some toast and the last of the marmalade. I needed to do some grocery shopping, but I had a suddenly free afternoon to take care of neglected domestic duties.

Homes for Hope was a local chapter of the national organization. After my first days in high tech it seemed only right to try and give something back. So I became a volunteer, and as I gained experience in plumbing I got to do more and more on the projects.

The house was nearing completion, nearly ready for a deserving family to move in and start a new life. It was why I donated my time — the idea that with each project I helped give one family a fresh start.

When I arrived at the house the dishwasher was ready to install, then the sink and garbage disposal. I checked in with Carl Adams, the project leader, and wormed my way into the base cabinet that would house the dishwasher.

A plumber spends a lot of time under sinks, or under houses. It gave me a unique perspective on the world, looking at the rest of the crew from their toes to about their knees. I got to know people by their shoes.

Carl's engineer boots, for instance. Well-worn black leather with straps and buckles around the ankles, they fit with who he was and what he did.

A pair of stiletto heels tapped into sight, shattering the early morning calm.

My mother. I had to stop thinking about people and making them appear; it was creeping me out.

"Georgiana? Are you under there? I saw your car, dear, and stopped to check on you. You never called me."

My mother's face appeared in the open face of the cabinet, upside down. "Georgiana?"

I waved her back and shimmied out. One thing you didn't do to Sandra Neverall was ignore her. It never worked out well.

"I'm sorry, Mom," I said, walking back toward the front of the house, away from the rest of the crew. "I got busy, and then it was late. I know how you hate for people to call late."

"Yes. But you're my daughter. You could call me." She picked a piece of imaginary lint off her impeccably tailored suit with her freshly manicured nails.

Plum Crazy. It had been my favorite color, in my manicure days, and it was a perfect description of how Mom made me feel.

"What brings you out here?" I asked. "Isn't it kind of early?"

She turned her wrist and glanced at a dainty gold watch I'd never seen before. The twinkle of diamonds surrounded the face, and she caught my appraising glance. "A gift," she said, before I could comment. "For my work on the Clackamas Commons Development."

A gift from Gregory, she meant. It was the sort of thing I would expect him to give her — shiny, expensive, and showy. Something that would publicly mark her as his property.

The same kind of gifts Blake used to give me; most of which ended up in a resale shop to fund my trip back to Oregon.

"Yes, it is a little early, but I have to go check on the subcontractors at the Commons. We're having a problem with the landscapers, and I wanted to straighten it out before I went to the office."

I nodded, and looked at my own battered plastic watch. "I really need to get back to work, Mom."

"Do you know what's really going on, Georgie? I heard that man *died* in the moat. And now the sheriff has closed the site indefinitely. Do you really think it's safe?" For a moment, my mother's façade cracked. I heard fear in her voice and saw real worry on her face.

"I don't know much, Mom. He was apparently out there in the middle of the night. There's no light, and it looks like he fell in the moat and drowned." I shook my head. "It's perfectly safe to work out there. We take all the necessary safety precautions. And we don't wander around in the dark."

I reached over and squeezed Mom's hand. There was a hint of looseness in the skin on the back of her hand, a reminder that she was getting older. Maybe she was feeling it, too.

She smiled at me, her relief clear. "I didn't know he was out there in the dark. All I've heard are rumors and gossip and some wild stories. This makes a lot more sense."

"It's okay, Mom. It was a stupid accident — sad for him and his friends and family, but an accident. Don't give it any more thought."

She nodded and punched the unlock button for her Escalade. "Have to go take care of the landscapers," she said.

She climbed into the driver's seat and pulled her seat belt across her shoulder. A lamb's-wool cover kept the belt from wrinkling her crisp white blouse. "We should have dinner again soon," she said before she started the car. "I'll call you."

"Not Tuesday," I reminded her. "Classes

start again on Tuesday." My mother had a habit of conveniently forgetting things she didn't want to acknowledge, like my plumbing classes at the community college.

I went back to work in the kitchen. From under the sink I was nearly invisible to the rest of the crew. I could hear the pounding of hammers and the occasional whine of a saw, but they sounded far away.

When the dishwasher was done, I got Carl to help me set the sink in place. Connecting the drains and feeds and installing the disposal took the rest of my shift, but I was done well before lunchtime.

I checked out with Carl, accepted his thanks for my work, and jumped into the Beetle. There was time to stop and see Paula before I had to go walk the dogs.

The library sat at one corner of the high school. Its white clapboard siding hadn't changed in as long as I could remember, and much longer than that, according to my mother.

I'd spent a lot of my afternoons hiding out in the cool stacks, avoiding the social ambitions my mother had for me. She thought I should be a cheerleader; I wanted to join the Computer Club. I compromised by doing neither. Instead I hung around the library and read a lot.

The late Martha Tepper had been the librarian then. Now Paula ran the library. A computer terminal had replaced the trays of checkout cards, but the carousel of stamps still sat on the desk behind the tall counter, and the basket for returns was in the same place on top of the counter.

There was something reassuring about the sameness of the library — a familiar place where I always felt welcome.

Paula was at her desk, a pair of reading glasses perched on the end of her nose. The glasses were a recent addition. She quickly pulled them off and tucked them in the pocket of her jacket when I came in.

It was the jacket that caught my attention. On the lapel was a familiar brooch. It had belonged to Martha Tepper and the elder librarian had worn it every day.

Paula caught my glance and gestured self-consciously at the brooch. "Janis said I should have it. That it belonged in the library."

"How is Janis?" I asked over my shoulder as I headed for the tiny kitchen at the back of the building. Paula kept the coffee on all day, and it was usually fresh. She drank it too fast for it to get stale.

"She's good," Paula said, following me back. "Getting used to being a woman of

120

means." Janis had inherited Miss Tepper's sizable estate.

"I'm sure she'll manage," I said lightly. "And what about you? How are you doing?"

"Better than you, from what I hear," she answered.

We took our coffee back up front, and Paula went back to tapping computer keys, logging in returns. It was second nature to her, and she kept up the conversation as she worked.

"Barry says you knew the guy that had the accident. That he was somebody you used to work with. Or something like that."

She was fishing for information. Clearly, Barry had said something that made her think there was more to the story. Maybe because there was.

I debated how much to tell her. I'd told Sue, but she was my oldest and best friend. Paula, though, was a close second.

"We worked together. It was complicated. We had a personal relationship as well as a business one, and it all ended very badly."

I paused to sip my coffee. Paula didn't say anything. She just waited for me to go on.

"It's not something I like to talk about. It was a bad time, it's over, and I put it behind me. Ancient history."

"Then what was he doing here?" Paula

glanced up from her typing long enough to give me a puzzled look. "I mean, if he was such ancient history, why was he in Pine Ridge?"

"According to what I heard, he was here on a job. Computer security for the Mc-Comb place."

Paula glanced up again. "Computer security? There weren't any computers. The place isn't even built yet!"

"There's a lot that can be done during construction," I said. I started to explain about wiring and shields and hard-wired systems.

Paula's eyes widened and I stopped talking.

"You really know all that, Georgie. You ought to be doing computer stuff, not being a plumber."

I shook my head. Something occurred to me and I narrowed my eyes. "How much has Barry told you?"

"Nothing really," she said quickly. "Just that you know a lot about computers, but you don't talk about it much."

I sighed. Secrets could be a real pain. "I used to work in high tech, okay? Been there, done that, got the T-shirt. Don't want to go back ever again."

"Whatever you say. But you know Pine

Ridge isn't exactly in the heart of the Silicone Rain Forest. I just think you've got some talents you keep hidden."

"Yeah, I'm a regular Jedi master of computers."

The sarcasm wasn't lost on Paula. "C'mon," she said. "You know there are people around here who'd welcome the help with that kind of stuff. If you ever change your mind . . ." She held her hands out, palms up.

"Thanks, but no thanks." I laughed. "But you can tell Barry you tried. He's still stuck with a lady plumber."

Paula blushed. "That wasn't Barry talking, that was me. I wish there was someone around here I could go to for help when this system goes haywire."

"Ooooh, I get it. You heard I helped Barry, and you want in on the deal. Why didn't you say so?"

"I admit I'd like the help," she said. "But I really think you could — oh, never mind. You're going to do exactly what you want, and nobody's going to change your mind." She chuckled. "If your mother couldn't, and Wade couldn't, what chance do I think I have?"

She was so right it made me laugh. "No chance, Paula. But if you have a problem, you can call me. As long as you don't mention it to anyone else. I'm really not interested in starting up my own company here."

Like my mother, I could conveniently forget things, too. I told Paula I wasn't interested in starting a business in Pine Ridge. So why was I interested in the empty storefront on Main Street that would make a great martial arts studio?

Paula and I visited a little longer. She didn't know anything more than I did about Blake's death, though we both agreed it had been a really dumb idea to go out to the McComb site in the dark.

On the way home, I turned on the radio in the Beetle, in time to catch the local newscast. Pine Ridge was too small to have their own station, but one of the Portland stations carried local news at noon.

I wasn't listening carefully as I pulled into my driveway, but the name *Pine Ridge* caught my attention. I waited with the engine idling while I listened to the rest of the item.

Although the short piece was carefully worded and gave no details, it was clearly about Blake. His identity was being withheld pending notification of next of kin.

According to the report, the investigation into the death was "ongoing," and the cause of death had not been released by the sheriff.

Now that was weird. Why wasn't the sheriff saying Blake had drowned? There didn't seem to be any reason not to.

I shut off the engine and shoved the keys in my pocket. I was nearly to the front door when a sheriff's cruiser pulled up at the foot of the driveway.

Deputy Carruthers unfolded his lanky frame from behind the wheel and intercepted me before I could unlock the door.

"Miss Neverall, could you come with me, please? The sheriff would like to talk to you."

I hesitated with my key inches from the lock. "Can it wait? I can drive myself after I let the dogs out. It will only be a few minutes."

Carruthers shifted his weight. His posture became more imposing, his presence sterner. "The sheriff said right away. Can the dogs wait?" The tone of his question told me the answer he expected.

I didn't disappoint him. I had a hunch it wouldn't have done me much good to argue anyway. "I'm sure they'll manage for a little longer."

"Good."

Carruthers led me back to the cruiser. He hesitated when we reached the car. Then he shrugged slightly, as though he had reached a decision, and opened the front door of the cruiser.

I took it as a good sign.

We drove to the sheriff's station in silence. Carruthers wasn't the talkative type, and I wasn't volunteering anything right now.

Not until I knew what this was all about.

CHAPTER 13

The atmosphere at the sheriff's station wasn't much different from the one in the cruiser.

Carruthers led me to a featureless room with an old desk and an office chair upholstered in cracked green vinyl. I'd been in this office before. The comfort level hadn't improved since my last visit.

He offered me a cup of coffee and said to wait. Sheriff Mitchell would be with me as soon as he could.

The coffee was bitter from sitting on a warmer plate too long. Just like I was sitting in that room too long. I was still wearing the coveralls I'd worn on the Hope house job that morning. Without a purse, I didn't even have a book to read while I waited.

I considered the consequences of just leaving and had about decided to take the chance when the sheriff finally appeared.

He pushed an ergonomically correct chair

into place behind the desk, sat down, and put his ever-present recorder in the middle of the desk.

"You mind?" he asked, waving at the recorder.

We'd had this conversation before. Not just the night before in my living room, but during the Tepper investigation. I could object, but Mitchell had proved himself a fair man.

I shrugged. "I suppose not. But I reserve the right to change my mind." I wanted to remind him I had done just that the night before and he had turned off the recorder.

"Of course." His voice was carefully neutral, but his manner was distant and his face guarded. His entire demeanor was decidedly chillier than it had been only a few hours earlier.

That, coupled with the fact he'd had me brought to the station instead of him coming to see me, set off warning bells.

Something was wrong. The lizard brain went into fight or flight mode, pumping adrenaline through my system. I had to struggle to remain still in the chair.

Focus. I had to focus.

I took a deep calming breath, just as the sensei had taught me. I made my mind overrule the irrational fears of my body, and brought my galloping heart under control.

The sheriff just looked at me, waiting for me to say something.

I forced myself to look back, to hold his gaze. He had me brought here, he could darned well tell me what this was about.

And I wasn't going to ask.

The corner of the sheriff's mouth twitched for a split second, as though he was amused by something. Or maybe I imagined it as a way to stifle my anxiety.

"I apologize for the delay," he said in a tone that wasn't at all apologetic. "I was in a meeting that ended up taking much longer than I expected."

He placed a manila folder on the desk and opened it, tilting the file so I couldn't see the contents. He might not know I could read it upside down, but he wasn't taking any chances.

"Miss Neverall, there are some questions that have come up about your relationship with the deceased, Mr. Weston."

The recorder clicked as he stopped talking. It was my turn, and it was clear this time he was going to leave the recorder running.

"Yes? What kind of questions?"

"It seems like you weren't completely up front with me about you and Blake Weston,

Miss Neverall."

"I told you the truth. We were business associates, we had a personal relationship, and it ended badly. I hadn't seen or spoken to the man for several years before he showed up here in Pine Ridge."

I sat back and crossed my arms. I pressed my lips tightly together. I wouldn't offer him anything more.

"Miss Neverall," the sheriff's tone was sharp, "you had a confrontation with Mr. Weston in front of the entire work crew just a few hours before he died. From what I hear, it sounded like a lot more than a bad breakup. Is there anything more you want to tell me about that?"

I didn't answer. My yelling at Blake had nothing to do with him falling in the moat. Did it?

The sheriff scribbled something in his file. Probably a note about the scowl I could feel spread across my face. The recorder wouldn't pick that up.

"Look," I said. My patience was shot, and I wanted to get home and let the dogs out while there was still a chance the carpets were intact. "You asked me all this yesterday, and I gave you answers. I told you about my history with Blake Weston. I admit, I thought he was a jerk and a liar, but he didn't deserve to die." I shuddered, remembering the Italian loafers toes-down in the mud.

"Nobody deserves to drown in a freakin' moat. But my argument with Blake had nothing to do with him being out there in the dark. If he came back out after I yelled at him, that was his stupidity. And no, nobody deserves to die just for being stupid, either."

I stopped and drew a deep breath. I could feel a flush spreading up my neck and across my face. I was suddenly too warm. I fanned myself with my hand.

"Sorry," I muttered.

"You don't have any idea what Mr. Weston was doing out at the McComb site?"

"He said he was there on a job — consulting on the security system."

"We knew that. I mean do you have any knowledge of why he was there specifically on Wednesday night. Anything he might have said? Anything in the way he worked that might explain why he was out there that night?"

"Not really. He said something about looking at the site without the client, but he was doing that in the morning. I have no idea why he would be back out."

Something wasn't right. Blake's death was

131

an accident — a stupid accident, but still an accident.

"Sheriff Mitchell," I unfolded my arms and leaned my forearms on the desk. "I don't understand why you're asking all these questions. Blake drowned. Right?"

The sheriff looked at the file in front of him, and tapped a finger against the pages. He glanced up at me a couple times, always returning to the file. It was like he was trying to decide exactly what to say.

I had the distinct impression that the answer — if he answered at all — was no.

"The cause of death has not been determined. The Medical Examiner wasn't available until early this afternoon. Until she has examined the body we can't say what might have happened."

Okay, not what I wanted to hear. Instead of having Doc Cox sign the death certificate, they had called in the county Medical Examiner. Never a good sign.

"Do you have anything you want to add to your statement, Miss Neverall? Any information that might be useful to us in our investigation?"

I shook my head. The sheriff looked from me to the recorder and back again, his eyebrow raised in a question.

"No," I said, for the benefit of the recorder. "I can't think of anything that would help. I wish I could." That last part was especially true. I would like nothing better than to give them some information that would get this over with.

"All right." He picked up the recorder and stuck it in his shirt pocket. "I'll have your statement typed up. Might take a little while."

I sighed. So much for the carpets. Buddha would at least use the tile at the back porch, but there was no telling how or where Daisy would exhibit her pique.

The sheriff looked at me, and came to some decision. His face settled into a stern expression. "I'll want you to come back in and sign the statement, and I may have more questions once we determine the cause of death. In the meantime, you're free to go."

I stood up and grabbed my jacket. "Thanks."

"Just don't plan any long-distance trips in the next few days. I have a feeling I'll need to talk to you again."

I nodded and hustled out the door before he could change his mind. I would come back and sign whatever he wanted, but I needed to get out of there.

I was out the door on the sidewalk before

I remembered I didn't have a car. Carruthers had picked me up in the cruiser.

I was stranded.

I supposed I could go back in and have someone drive me home — but right now I didn't want to go in that office for any reason. The sheriff was suspicious about me and Blake, and he wouldn't say Blake had drowned.

Which probably meant he hadn't.

I refused to consider that possibility. Of course he had drowned. It was the only explanation I could accept. The alternatives were unthinkable.

It was only a few blocks to Sue's shop — two blocks over to Main and a couple blocks down — and I wasn't sure where else to go. Wade might be in his office, but what would I say to him?

I shrugged into my jacket, feeling the weight of my cell phone bump against my side. If Sue wasn't there I could call someone for a ride.

Like who? If I called Wade I would have to explain how I got downtown without my car. And he wasn't going to believe for a second that I was just out for a walk — without the dogs.

My mom? The thought made me cringe. Whatever I didn't want to tell Wade, I wanted to tell my mother even less.

To my relief, Sue was in the shop when I arrived. She looked up with a puzzled expression. She obviously hadn't heard the Beetle pull up in front, and I was wearing work coveralls.

"I walked," I said, as though that explained everything.

Her brows knit in confusion. "What?"

"I walked," I repeated as I closed the door behind me. "But only from the sheriff's office."

She shot me a disgusted look. "You're just messing with me, aren't you?"

I grinned at her. "Maybe a little. But I really was at the sheriff's office and I did walk over here."

There was no one in the shop, and I was grateful for the chance to talk privately. "He had more questions about Blake. Had Carruthers come out to the house and 'offer' me a ride to the station. It sounded like one of those offers you shouldn't refuse." I waved a hand in the general direction of the sheriff's office. "I got done a few minutes ago, so now I need a ride home."

Sue blinked a couple times, as though trying to piece together what I'd said. She looked the way I felt when I talked to her — like she'd just stepped into the middle of a completely different conversation.

"Back up," she said. "Let's try this again."

I laughed out loud. Usually it was me telling her to start over and explain what she was talking about.

"What's funny?" Sue demanded. "The sheriff had you dragged down to his office to answer questions, and then he didn't even have someone drive you home? I mean, all those cop shows, they always have an officer drive the person home. It's like standard procedure or something, isn't it?"

"Maybe he would have thought of it, if I'd stuck around," I admitted. "But I was in a hurry to get out. I don't even know why, really. It was just strange and uncomfortable, and I wanted to leave more than I wanted a ride home."

Sue glanced up at the clock. It was a kitschy big-eyed cat that she'd found at a garage sale a couple years ago. I'd told her what it was worth as a collectible, but she insisted she didn't care and it stayed on her wall.

"It's not really closing time yet, but nothing's happening here. Why don't we go walk the dogs, and you can tell me what happened."

It sounded good to me.

CHAPTER 14

Sue parked her SUV in the driveway behind the Beetle. From inside we could hear excited yelps. They knew the sound of the Beetle, but they also knew Sue's vehicle and that it always carried the promise of green treats.

Sue didn't disappoint them. After she gave them treats she let them out the back door, while I dumped the coveralls and grabbed a pair of jeans and a sweater.

Once I was changed we got the leashes and headed out. The weather had turned cool, and the trees were a riot of golds and reds. Soon they would be bare, but for now we could admire the display of autumn color.

The falling leaves also created interesting new smells for the dogs to explore. Daisy alternately dawdled and sprinted, checking out every leaf. Buddha was less erratic. He methodically stopped and examined each spot that caught his attention before moving on at the same deliberate pace.

Their initial enthusiasm waned and they fell into the steady rhythm of the walk. With the dogs under control, Sue started in on me.

"Georgie, if Fred Mitchell had you brought to the station, he had a good reason. Just what's going on?" She reached out and touched my arm. "Don't get upset. I know you like to keep your secrets. And I try to respect that. But don't you think it's about time you started trusting somebody?"

"You're taking his side?" I asked. I knew she and the sheriff were becoming an item, but clearly she was further gone than I thought.

"Sides?" Sue threw one hand — the one without the leash — in the air in a gesture of frustration. "What is this, second grade?! Nobody's taking sides here, Georgie. I just think there has to be a reason, that's all."

She stopped and glared at me. "And you keep brushing off my questions. Just like you kept brushing me off when I wanted to come visit you in San Francisco.

"It's like your entire life is some big secret that we're not allowed to know about, and it's really frustrating."

"Your friend the sheriff hauls me down to

his office, strands me in town, and you defend him and then say you aren't taking sides?"

"Georgie, this isn't about that, and you know it. What I said was that Fred wouldn't call you in without a reason, and I wanted you to tell me what the reason was."

She tugged Buddha's leash to hurry him up. He responded obediently and picked up his pace. They drew away from me and Daisy, and I was left with Sue's hurt voice ringing in my ears.

She had taken Fred Mitchell's side. She'd defended him without even knowing exactly what happened at the station. What's worse was that she was right.

I hustled Daisy along in spite of her protests and caught up to Sue and Buddha.

"I'm sorry," I said. "I hate it when you're right and I'm wrong," I added, trying to lighten the mood.

Sue shrugged. "You have a lot of secrets, Georgie. Maybe it's time you started sharing what's going on."

It was my turn to shrug. "There really isn't anything *going on,* Sue. The sheriff had some questions. I just thought he was being a little high-handed."

"What kind of questions, that's what I want to know. What was so important to him that he had Carruthers haul you down there? I mean, he'd been out to the house to talk to you just last night, right?"

"How did you know he'd been to the house?"

Sue colored. "He, uh, stopped by to talk to me after he left your place. He might have mentioned that he'd seen you."

"Was he asking you about me? Or was this a purely social visit? What's up between the two of you?"

We were a few blocks from my house, and the dogs knew it. They strained at the leashes — as much as Buddha ever misbehaved — anxious to get home and get another treat.

"You hungry?" Sue asked, her conversation taking another of its patented abrupt turns. This one, I suspected, had a lot less to do with her conversational style and a lot more with not talking about Fred Mitchell.

I wasn't going to let her off the hook that easily, but just then my stomach rumbled loudly.

Sue took that as an answer. "Let's get the dogs home and then we can go grab a sandwich at Franklin's."

I shook my head. "Not Franklin's. Not Tiny's, either. In fact, I don't want to go anywhere in Pine Ridge. Nowhere that I

140

might run into anybody I know."

We walked the rest of the way, running through a list of not-so-local joints until we settled on a Mexican place about twenty miles away. It wasn't a long drive, but it put just enough distance between me and Pine Ridge.

I wondered if the sheriff would approve of my "leaving town" and decided I didn't care. Sue volunteered to drive, and I accepted her offer. Much as I loved my old Beetle, her SUV was a lot more comfortable.

I cranked up the stereo and let twenty-year-old rock music fill the car. It made conversation nearly impossible. Sue didn't object. We both were avoiding the discussion we knew was coming: my confessions about Blake and Samurai Security, and Sue's relationship with Fred Mitchell.

We needed to talk. We both knew it. Ever since I'd returned to Pine Ridge I had maintained a distance, even with the people I was closest to like Sue and Wade. I was starting to relax a little, but the Blake situation was pushing things along.

I'd grown used to keeping secrets. Attending one of the most competitive schools in the country had required me to be self-sufficient, but it was nothing compared to working in an industry that ran on trade secrets and innovation. Secrecy and security were the standard, and nondisclosure agreements accompanied every move.

Paranoia was a survival tactic that pervaded the industry, and as a security firm it was the foundation of our business. After a while keeping secrets just came naturally.

Sue pulled into the nearly empty parking lot and braked to a stop in a Saint Doris parking place. It was a designation we had learned as kids watching Doris Day movies on TV with Sue's mom. Doris never had to look for a parking place. There was always an empty spot right in front just waiting for her. Sue's mom had started invoking the name of Saint Doris when she drove us anywhere, and we had carried on the tradition.

The restaurant was as empty as the parking lot. The food was great, but lunch was several hours past and the dinner crowd was at least an hour away.

I breathed a sigh of relief. We could talk in private.

We settled into a booth with menus, a basket of chips, and a bowl of salsa. The waiter appeared a moment later with water and an offer of drinks.

Sue gave me a quick look and ordered a

margarita and a diet soda, then sent the waiter away. I furrowed my brow. She never had so much as a sip of wine if she was driving.

"The margarita's for you, girl. You look like you could use it. I'm having soda."

I was tempted to argue with her, but I'd tried that already today and it didn't work very well. "Yes, ma'am."

She laughed. "I never have to twist very hard when there's tequila involved," she said.

It was an old joke. I seldom drank anything stronger than microbrew, but when I did it usually did involve tequila. Sue knew my weaknesses.

"Thanks. I think maybe I could use one."

Our drinks arrived, Sue's in an ice-filled tumbler and mine in a saucer-shaped glass with a rim of rock salt. I think I liked the salt as much as the drink.

The waiter took our order and disappeared, leaving us facing the conversation we'd been dancing around for the last several days.

"Sooo," Sue said, drawing the word out. "Just what did Fred Mitchell want with you? I mean, you hadn't seen this guy in several years, right? Then he has a stupid accident in your hometown. Not much to tell."

"That's what I thought, but there is more." I sighed and sipped the margarita, tasting the sharp bite of lime and the tang of salt, feeling the warmth of tequila hitting my empty stomach and spreading through me.

I relaxed a little and set the drink aside. No more tequila on an empty stomach.

"Sue, I have never talked to anyone about everything that happened down there and I hoped I'd never have to. It was an unhappy time, and I just wanted it to go away. I really hoped it would stay in the past."

She nodded. "Understood."

"Now it looks like I have to tell somebody and try to figure out how much I have to tell everybody else. But I have to have your word that you won't repeat this to anyone, including Fred Mitchell." It was my turn to give her a hard look. "*Especially* Fred Mitchell."

"What is this fixation with me and Fred Mitchell?" She tried to sound like injured innocence, but I didn't believe her.

I ticked off the clues on my fingers. "First, you blush every time his name is mentioned. Second, he just happens to drop by and talk to you at home. Third, you're calling him by his name instead of *sheriff.* And fourth, you act guilty every time I ask about him." I waved a hand. "Do I need to go on?"

She shook her head. "No. We've gone out a couple times is all. He did stop to ask me about you, what I knew about San Francisco. That was when I realized how little I *did* know."

She drew a deep breath and went on. "And when have I ever snitched on you for anything? Did I tell anybody about you kissing Eddie Monroe in fifth grade? And that kegger our senior year, even after I got caught? Not a word. So why would I do it now?"

"Because you have a thing for the sheriff," I shot back.

I held up my hands in surrender before we could escalate into another argument. "But I get your point. You don't snitch."

"Try to remember that."

"Ouch. You're right. But I know what kind of dumb moves you can make when there's a guy involved." I swallowed hard. This was it.

"Let me tell you how I know."

Our food arrived. Sue took a bite of her enchilada and waited patiently for me to go on. I picked up my taco but I didn't eat. Instead I tried to figure out where to start.

"It's hard to admit a failure, Sue — even harder when you're the person who always succeeded, the kid that got straight As and went to the best university.

"San Francisco was a spectacular failure."

I took a bite of taco and stared at my plate as I chewed. The worst was over. I'd said the f-word. Now all I had to do was explain how stupid I'd been because of a guy.

Piece of cake.

The taco seemed to stick in my throat and I swallowed hard to force it down. "When I graduated the computer industry was booming. There were jobs everywhere and my degrees put me in high demand." I took a sip of margarita, letting the frigid liquid soothe my tightening throat.

"That's not bragging — it's a fact. I had offers from all over the country. But I wanted to be in the middle of it, and I decided to take a job in the Bay Area.

"It didn't take me long to realize I wanted to be the boss. So I started my own company. It was just me at first, and I named it Samurai Security." I saw Sue's mouth twitch with the hint of a smile.

"I know." I grinned just a little. "But I loved the martial arts I'd been studying since college and somehow the idea of an ancient samurai warrior protecting a client's computer appealed to me."

"It fits you," Sue said.

"Yeah. Well, I had some early success and my clients started recommending me to their friends and pretty soon I had more work than I could handle. I went looking for a partner to help share the workload. Word got out I was looking, and people started coming to me, recommended by friends, and friends of friends.

"That's when I found Blake." I shrugged. "Or when Blake found me."

Sue's eyes widened. "Oh."

"Yeah. Oh. Even after all that happened I have to admit he was impressive. Ivy League degrees, good dresser, charming, and — I have to say — gorgeous. Not my usual type, but I'm not sure I actually had a type at the time."

Sue gave me a questioning look, which seemed to shout "What about Wade?", but I waved it away. "Which is beside the point right now. Anyway, he was gorgeous in a suave, man-about-town way. Not a rugged alpha-male-I'm-the-sheriff way."

I grinned at Sue, and she blushed. There was definitely something going on there. There wasn't time right now, but I would eventually get the truth out of her.

"Long and short of it, Blake had all the qualities to be an excellent salesman and company rep. Plus he was scary smart and he knew his way around a security design.

"In a word, *perfect.*"

I ate a couple bites of my now-cool food before I went on.

"We worked together — long hours, no breaks, take-out lunches and dinners, and way too much coffee. It was an intense atmosphere. We spent most of the time together, and there wasn't a week that we worked less than a hundred hours."

Sue's expression was stunned. "Hundred-hour weeks? That doesn't sound like a lot of fun."

"I don't know if I'd call it fun, but it was exciting. We were creating a company out of nothing but our brains and energy, we were being successful, and it was moving fast."

I took another sip of my margarita. It was partially melted, the lime not as tart, the tequila less intense.

"Too fast, it turned out. We grew as much as we could with just the two of us. I had every penny tied up in the company, and that was when my dad died."

"I remember you coming home for the funeral. You looked terrible. At the time I figured it was losing your dad, but it sounds like there was more to it."

"Gee thanks," I said sarcastically. Then I smiled. "You're right, I was exhausted and I was afraid to be away. Every day I was gone cost Samurai money. Blake was working too many hours already. He couldn't cover his work and mine, too.

"And then it turned out Mom needed money."

Sue nodded. "That was one thing I never understood. I mean, we all hear how rich doctors are."

"If they're getting paid, maybe. But if they're treating patients for free . . ."

"For free?"

"He wasn't billing the loggers who were laid off, or their families. It's a long story.

"Anyway" — I went back to my confession — "she needed money, and I had every penny tied up in Samurai. Blake and I talked it over and decided we needed investors to be able to expand — and maybe I could get some cash out of the deal to help my mom."

Sue pushed her empty plate away. "It sounds like there is a but at the end of that sentence."

I sighed. "There is. We found some venture capital that came with several strings. We ended up with a board of directors who wanted to run things, and we let them. Even so, by the time I actually had some cash in hand, Mom had started working for Gregory and was determined not to take charity from her daughter."

"That explains a whole lot about your mom," Sue said.

I nodded. "It certainly does. It makes her crazy that I volunteer at Homes for Hope. But that's another story.

"Things in San Francisco were good for a while. We had people to take care of the business stuff, and I could concentrate on the actual computer and security issues. I did some work that I'm still proud of.

"At the direction of the board, we went through the process of selling stock, and Blake and I got some very lucrative stock options." I grinned. "That's where the convertible came from. Cashed some of my first stock options and bought it. We were on top of the world for a while. Even had time for a social life, sort of. That was when Blake and I got to be a serious couple."

The waiter appeared, whisking away the empty plates, and bringing Sue a refilled soda. I waved away his offer of a second drink, and slid my half-eaten lunch his direction.

"I don't know when it all went bad, exactly. We were too busy playing hard and working even harder to notice.

"The board wanted to move away from

our core business, add a retail security division, and a hardware development group. They insisted we could expand without losing our market. I disagreed with them and Blake disagreed with me. I thought we should focus on what we were good at, and we were already grossing several million dollars a year, but Blake kept saying we had to grow or die. We argued about it a lot."

"Is that what broke you up?"

"I really don't know," I admitted. "I just know he called me late one night and left a nasty message on my voice mail. I tried to call him to find out what was wrong, but he wouldn't talk to me."

"A breakup over voice mail? Yow. That's cold."

"It gets worse. Stan Fischer called me early the next morning. He was a real hands-on member of the board, and he said he had to see me before the board meeting. He offered me the opportunity to resign before the board fired me."

"But it was your company! That's not right."

"Remember what I said about those stock sales? The board was in control. Not me. Blake had always been better at the office politics than I was, and I figured he'd known which way to jump.

"I can take a hint. Eventually. Stan was giving me the chance to salvage a little dignity out of the situation, so I signed the resignation letter and went home to pack. I let them steal the company out from under me."

Sue had picked up the check. When I reached for it to figure my share she held it out of my reach. "After that," she said, "I'll get the check. Besides, I'm the one who ordered the margarita. You can get the tip."

I looked at the margarita glass, still half full of melted ice that turned the drink a pale anemic green. I left the glass on the table and walked out.

CHAPTER 15

All the way home Sue kept glancing over at me. I knew she had more questions, but I was drained. I had poured out the long, sad story of Colossal Failure Georgiana Neverall and I had nothing more to say.

Sue parked her SUV in my driveway and shut off the engine. "Is there anything I can do, Georgie? I can only imagine how awful this is for you." She turned to face me in the dark car. "Besides, I don't think you failed. Look at it this way. You built a successful company, hired good people, and attracted investors.

"I mean, the company had to be *worth* stealing, didn't it?"

I had no answer for her. I had never looked at the events in that light. It didn't make the loss of Samurai any less painful, but it did ease the cloud that hung over all my memories of San Francisco. Just as long as I didn't think about Blake.

That was the ultimate betrayal, and it still hurt.

I leaned across and gave Sue an awkward hug. "I don't know why that should make me feel better, but it does. I just never thought of it that way."

"Well start," she said.

I climbed out of the car and headed inside. I heard Sue back out and pull away as I locked the front door behind me.

I was exhausted.

I let the dogs out, and dumped a load of coveralls and heavy socks into the washer. No matter how stressed out I was, I still needed clothes for work.

By the time the clothes were ready for the dryer I was ready for bed. I ignored the rest of the housework, thankful I lived alone. No one would check if there were dust bunnies under the bed when I fell into it.

I knew there were more ghosts lurking, and more revelations would be necessary. But for tonight I was just too tired to worry about any of them.

When I woke up the next morning I felt great. For about fourteen seconds. Then I remembered that Blake was dead, Stan Fischer was coming to Pine Ridge, the sheriff was asking prying questions, and I'd told Sue the ugly truth about my years in San Francisco.

It was not quite daylight but I couldn't get back to sleep — the downside of falling asleep at nine o'clock. There was nothing to be done for it but crawl out of bed and stagger to the bathroom.

Maybe things would look better after a hot shower.

At least they looked brighter, if only because the sun was coming up.

The message light was blinking on the answering machine. It was always blinking lately. I didn't want to talk to anybody, and I let the messages stack up until they threatened to fill the memory.

I started a pot of coffee and pushed the message button. My mother had called multiple times, each a little more perturbed than the last. She was genuinely concerned, although there was a part of me that always wondered if it was me she was concerned about, or how I reflected on her.

Wade had called, just to check in. He apparently didn't know about my second visit to the sheriff's office. I added him to the list of people I had to tell before they heard it somewhere else.

Barry had called about the time I'd gone to bed. He'd had a call from Sheriff Mitchell, and the McComb site was still off-limits. He said to call him in the morning and he'd let me know if there was work. He didn't sound optimistic.

Paula had called, too. And Richard Parks again, just to make sure I wouldn't rat him out to Stan. By then I was listening to just a few seconds before deleting each message.

I almost missed the one I'd been dreading.

"Hey there, Georgie Girl," a familiar voice boomed from the speaker. I hated that name — something about a pop song from before I was born — but Stan always used it. When I protested, he told me it was all about a girl who needed to lighten up. "Written just for you," he'd say.

I figured Stan to be about sixty, but it was hard to tell. He had been a kind of father figure at Samurai — if my father had lacked education and social skills — and he knew how to make money. I was still grateful to him for allowing me the chance to resign instead of getting fired and I suspected he'd done it without the board's knowledge.

I still didn't want anyone from Samurai in Pine Ridge, but after my talk with Sue I felt better about the fact that someone was going to pick up where Blake left off.

The booming voice surprisingly brought

back good memories and I decided it was probably better that it was Stan. I knew Stan, I could talk to him. I let myself feel a tiny ray of hope.

I made note of Stan's cell phone number and the name of his hotel in Portland. There wasn't anywhere in Pine Ridge that was appropriate for someone like Stan to stay.

I waited for the sun to climb above the horizon before I called Barry, and considered what to do with the day, if I didn't have to work.

The plumbing was finished at the Homes for Hope house, though I could help on other parts of the project. I looked around the kitchen. There was a backlog of housework that would keep me busy.

First, though, I had to find out whether Barry needed me.

Barry answered on the second ring. "I don't know when we'll get back out to McComb," he told me. "The sheriff isn't telling me anything about how long he needs to have the site closed."

I heard a heavy sigh on Barry's end. "I have a couple other little jobs, but they're already fully staffed. I don't really have anything for you. You might as well take a three-day weekend."

"Sure," I answered. What else could I say?

I'd already told him I had the month covered, which was only a slight exaggeration.

Besides, it was my last free Saturday. With classes starting again my Tuesday evenings and Saturday mornings were booked for the next three months.

I hung up. So what would it be? Clean house? See what Carl could find for me at Homes for Hope? A long drive with the top down?

I glanced at the weather and rejected the idea of a drive in the toy. It sounded like a great idea, except for the strong threat of rain.

I stalled by hauling out my *gi* and going through a complete workout. It calmed my nerves and stretched my muscles at the same time, leaving me relaxed and centered.

I thought again about the vacant storefront on Main Street. It had been a dance studio when I was a kid, full of the kind of little girls my mother wanted me to be.

A few minutes later I was in the Beetle, heading for Main Street. I had no money and no idea how I'd get a sensei to teach, but I wanted to look at that space again.

I nearly chickened out. It meant going downtown — as much downtown as there was in Pine Ridge — and possibly seeing people I didn't want to see. Still, it beat doing housework. My mother would be ashamed of me.

The sidewalk was empty when I parked the Beetle at the curb and climbed out. The brown paper was still taped over the front window, as it had been for months. One corner had come loose, and if I stood on tiptoe I could see into the dark interior.

There wasn't a lot to see. A scarred-wood floor, bare walls with ballet barres along one side, and two doors at the back. As I recalled, one door led to a tiny kitchen space just big enough for a sink and a miniature refrigerator. The other opened to a locker room of sorts and a bathroom. There was no need for separate spaces for girls and boys; when I grew up in Pine Ridge boys did not take dance lessons.

There was a fading "For Rent" sign in the front window.

There was no way I could afford it. I took my PDA out of my purse and made a note of the phone number anyway. Something told me I would need it eventually.

Sure. Right about the time I got a flying car.

I was standing on tiptoe again, staring in the corner of the window, when my mother called my name.

I dropped down onto flat feet and whirled

159

around. Of all the people I didn't want to see, two of them were standing just a few feet away — Mother and Gregory. Where did they come from?

"Hello, Georgiana," Mom said. She moved closer and stretched out to give me a peck on the cheek.

Her glance traveled down my outfit: plain blue T-shirt, a fleece jacket, jeans, and sneakers. She was wearing a smartly tailored suit and her trademark stilettos, even on a quiet Friday morning. Her expression made it clear my fashion choices did not meet with her approval.

"Working today?" she asked, looking me up and down again.

She knew I wore coveralls for work, but it was her way of expressing her disappointment with my wardrobe.

I bit back a snappish reply. I was standing here thinking about a martial arts studio, a place I went to learn control and serenity. Not the time or place for angry retorts.

"Day off," I said. "Didn't this used to be the dance studio?" As if I didn't remember vividly the flocks of girls in their frilly dance costumes waiting for their mothers to pick them up after class.

"You know, I think you're right." As if she didn't remember distinctly the arguments

160

over whether or not I would enroll in one of the tap or ballet classes. "I think it closed a few years ago. Not enough parents willing to keep their children enrolled."

Not enough parents able to afford it, more likely. But let her believe what she wanted. It wasn't worth arguing over.

"We were just headed into Dee's for a late breakfast when I saw you standing here," Mom said, motioning toward Gregory. He had walked back down the street and waited by Dee's door.

"Why don't you join us — at least for a little while? I haven't had a chance to talk to you in ages!"

I looked down the block to where Gregory waited. "Oh, Mom. You've already got company for breakfast. You don't need me horning in."

"Nonsense." She linked her arm through mine as though I had accepted her invitation. "Come on, it'll be fun."

I bit back the impulse to ask her to define *fun,* because breakfast with her and Gregory did not fall into any definition I had ever encountered.

"Well," I said hesitantly, "for a few minutes."

I walked the short distance to Dee's Lunch, arm in arm with my mother. She probably thought I'd run if she didn't hang on to me. And she might have been right. The thought did cross my mind, but if I did there would be consequences. There were always consequences with my mother.

Gregory held the door for us. His expression was anything but welcoming, however. He looked grumpy, an expression that seldom creased his polished and controlled exterior. Gregory always wore his salesman face in public.

The booths were designed for two, but Gregory led us to the back where the last booth added a straight chair in the dead-end part of the aisle.

"You sit there, Sandy," he said to my mother, waving at the marginally more comfortable-looking bench. "I'll take the chair."

I took the booth seat across from my mother, and Gregory pulled the chair up against the end of the table. I was effectively trapped in the booth.

For an instant I wondered how my mother had managed to come along at just the right moment to find me in the middle of Main Street, hijack me for breakfast, and trap me in a tiny booth in the back of Dee's Lunch with her and Gregory.

I dismissed the idea with a mental shudder. I needed to limit the number of paranoid fantasies I entertained at any one time, and Blake's death had already used up several weeks' worth. This one was ridiculous.

Mother and Gregory, despite their claims of going to breakfast, just ordered toast and coffee. I did the same in the hopes that signaled a brief stay.

Gregory carried the heavy china mugs from the counter and placed them ceremoniously on the table, as though he was presenting a fine wine.

Mom looked at him and said thanks, and I tried my best not to look at her. The goofy smile on her face gave me the oogies.

I had learned the hard way what happens when you trust a man with your finances and your heart, and I was afraid my mother was making the same mistake with Gregory. There was no way I could explain to her why I was worried, and no way she would believe me if I tried.

The conversation quickly went exactly where I didn't want it to go — Blake Weston and his untimely death.

"Georgiana —" Gregory's expression was somber. He looked like a mourner at a funeral for someone he didn't really know. He was serious because he should be, but he wasn't actually grieving.

"You knew the man that died out at the construction site, right? I heard he was from San Francisco. What was he doing out here in Pine Ridge?"

I took a deep breath. I remembered my morning workout and the sense of calm it had given me. I needed all the control I could get right now.

I turned to Gregory and spoke in a quiet voice. "I knew him several years ago, when I lived in the Bay Area. We worked together. I hadn't seen him in years. He said he was here on a job, as security consultant for Chad McComb."

He sipped his coffee, watching me over the rim of his mug. I held his gaze. I was not going to let Gregory Whitlock upset me again.

"Seems like a long way to come for a job. Aren't there any security consultants around here? Or in Seattle?"

I smiled briefly, lifting the corners of my mouth in a meaningless gesture. "I don't know why Chad hired him instead of getting someone local," I replied. "But I do know he was one of the best. I suppose when you're spending the kind of money McComb is, you get the best."

"True." Gregory paused as though he was

considering my answer, but I had the distinct impression he'd had his questions ready. "But he's hired all local people for the rest of the project. Why bring in someone from out of town for this part?"

Annoyance overrode control for a second. "Computer security is a highly technical and difficult field. I'd expect Chad McComb to have equipment that goes beyond state-of-the-art to protect sensitive data." I'd heard Chad still consulted for one of the big firms in Seattle. Sensitive didn't begin to describe the data he might have access to.

I reined in my temper before I disclosed how much I really knew about security. No one needed to know, especially Gregory.

"I'm sure Chad still had connections in the industry. Someone probably recommended Blake Weston."

I wondered if Gregory was really this ignorant, or if there was some other reason for his questions. I glanced at my mother, trying to figure out what her role in all this was.

"Have you heard anything, Mom?"

She shrugged, lifting her narrow shoulders a fraction of an inch. "No more than you have." She turned to Gregory. "Did the sheriff say anything when you talked to him?"

I glanced quickly at Gregory. He'd talked to the sheriff?

"The sheriff talked to you about Blake's death?" I asked.

"No," he said. "I stopped in to report some vandalism out at the Commons. Minor stuff, but I always have to make a police report for the insurance company.

"He was pretty closemouthed about the accident. Made me curious."

I tried to accept his explanation at face value, although I wasn't convinced. But if he wasn't going to offer any other explanation, I would gladly let the subject drop.

CHAPTER 16

We sat in silence for another minute or two, and I was about to ask Gregory to let me out when my mother spoke up.

"What were you looking for at the old dance studio, Georgiana? Maybe I can help you. We" — she waved her hand to include Gregory — "know the owners. It's been empty for more than a year, so I might be able to get you a good deal."

Her eyes sparkled, and she grew animated. "It would need some remodeling, I know. But you know the contractors now. I'm sure you could work something out."

I shook my head, confused by her sudden enthusiasm. "Work something out for what?"

"For your office, or shop, or whatever you call it. You know, the computer business. It's a wonderful idea!"

"Computer business?" I repeated. This was starting to feel like a conversation with

Sue, and I clearly hadn't had enough coffee to follow what she was saying.

"Of course. Isn't that what you were looking at the space for? It's a prime location, right on Main Street, with parking in front and the municipal lot one block over.

"Just think, Georgiana. Finally you could put that fancy degree to work!"

I squinted at her. She had jumped to several conclusions — all of them wrong — and gone into her sales pitch.

"Why would I want to start a computer business?" I asked.

Been there, done that, I added silently. Barely got out with the T-shirt on my back.

"You went to college for a lot of years, Georgiana. I would think you would want to use the knowledge you gained."

She didn't need to add the next sentence, the one I had heard all too often. The knowledge my father had paid all that money for. She conveniently forgot the jobs I'd held to help with expenses, and that I'd paid for grad school myself.

This was an argument that had been repeated so many times I could carry on both sides from memory.

She didn't understand why I had to go away to college. I couldn't wait to leave Pine Ridge. She thought Caltech was too expensive. I got grants and scholarships and loans to reduce the financial burden on her and Dad.

She thought I should find a good man and get married. I wanted an MS more than a Mrs.

The only thing worse than getting the fancy degrees was not using them to make money. Been there, done that, too. Saying it didn't work out quite the way I'd hoped was the understatement of the century.

We were all ready to sing the same song, about the millionth verse, but there was really no sense in having the discussion again. Nothing would change, and all we would gain was hurt feelings — hers and mine.

Better to let her keep her illusions for a while longer. Especially with my finances. About the only thing I could afford to start was an argument.

"We'll see," I said, unconsciously echoing her standard answer when she didn't want to say no. "It's just an idea right now, until I'm in a little better financial shape."

I grinned at her, hoping she would let it go for now. "But when I'm ready I'll be sure to give you a call."

I glanced at my watch — the good gold one today, since I wasn't working — and made a shocked face. "I had no idea it was getting so late! Gregory, could you let me out, please? I have some errands I need to take care of this morning, and I've dawdled here far too long already."

For one long moment I thought he was going to say no. He didn't move for several seconds. He finally relaxed, though it appeared to take an effort, and slid the chair aside.

"I already took care of it," he said, as I pulled some bills from my pocket.

"Thanks. Next time will be on me." I suppose I meant it. I just hoped there wouldn't be a next time. Fat chance.

I hadn't lied to Mom and Gregory. I did have several errands, although I didn't have to do them today.

I'd promised myself I would improve my cooking habits. The first step was a trip to the supermarket. I drove the mile or so to the local market and went to work on my new plan to cook dinner at home — at least a *couple* nights a week.

I stocked up on canned soup and packaged meal makers. It wasn't gourmet fare by any stretch of the imagination, but at least I was making an effort.

The refrigerator was empty, so I added some staples like eggs and milk and butter.

Some cheese — the individually wrapped slices we'd called *shingles* in college — peanut butter and jelly, and a fresh jar of marmalade.

I got dog food and paper towels.

A real Susie Homemaker. I blame it on spending the morning with my mother.

I felt all warm and cozy taking my bags out to the Beetle and stowing them in the front-end trunk. I had taken my time, but I was settling into my new role as a small-town single.

Talking with Sue had been a good idea. I was more relaxed and felt more connected than I had since I returned from San Francisco.

Pine Ridge was a small town, but it was *my* small town.

Which was what I thought until my cell phone rang as I was climbing into the driver's seat.

I glanced at the caller ID, having had enough of my mother for one morning. It was the number for the library.

"Hi, Paula." I put the key in the ignition but I waited to start the car. I didn't have a hands-free phone, so I usually didn't talk while I was driving.

"Georgie? Hi. Where are you?"

"I went to the grocery store, but I was just

171

getting in the car to go home. What do you need?"

"It's not me, actually, it's Barry. He's here. He went by your house but the Beetle was gone, and he asked me to call you. Can you stop by on your way home?"

"I guess so. Can't stay long. I have a trunk full of food that needs to get in the refrigerator."

"Okay. I'll see you in a few."

I hung up and started the engine. Paula had sounded strained, not her usual sunny self. And she wanted me to stop by right now, even though my trunk was full of groceries.

I concentrated on not thinking about what Barry wanted. If he was looking for me like this, it couldn't be good.

I thought about Paula instead. We had known each other in school, though she was a few years older, and we'd become friends in the months since I'd moved back to Pine Ridge. I wondered why she'd kept her maiden name and one of these days I was going to ask her about it.

Knowing Paula, there was a story attached. There was always a story with Paula. She loved telling stories and her favorites were of the touching love-story variety. Her life with Barry seemed to fit right in.

172

Barry's pickup was parked in front of the library, so I pulled around the corner and parked in the lot. The small clapboard building sat on the corner of the high school, and from across the parking lot I could see a crowd of teenagers milling around and calling to each other. Must be lunchtime.

I locked the Beetle, grateful for the cool weather. The milk, cheese, and butter would be okay for a little while.

Inside, the library looked like it always did, except for the bulky man in the heavy boots behind the counter. He looked very much out of place.

"Hi, Georgie. Thanks for stopping by." Barry picked up a mug off the desk, and gave Paula's shoulder a squeeze. "Come on back and have a cup of coffee."

It occurred to me that Barry could have just called me to the office, but had chosen to track me down instead. It was looking worse with each passing minute. I mentally started calculating whether I could live on unemployment benefits. Maybe Mom was right, I should start doing computer work. At least it would keep the dogs fed.

I followed Barry into the tiny kitchen in the back, and poured myself a cup from Paula's never-empty coffee pot.

173

Barry set his cup down and leaned against the counter, his arms crossed over his chest.

I stood near the back door, even though it was never opened and couldn't really provide an escape. I held my mug with both hands, my cold hands drawing warmth from the hot liquid.

"I need to talk to you, Georgie."

"I figured that, Bear." I used his nickname, and hoped this could be one of those "big brother" moments.

"If you have to lay me off I'll understand. Honest."

"Lay you off? Whatever gave you that crazy idea?"

"I know you're short of work with the sheriff keeping the McComb site shut down." I swallowed hard. "Has he given you any idea when we can get back to work?"

"Well I think I have enough work to keep everyone going for a while. I just need to shuffle some schedules. A couple of the guys wanted to take vacation anyway, since hunting season opened and now I can let 'em.

"That's not the problem."

"It isn't? I thought that was why you called me to come here, instead of the office. You wanted to give me the news in private. And I appreciate that," I added quickly.

"Well I am not laying you off. But you're right about the McComb site. That's a problem. As of an hour ago the sheriff has officially declared it a crime scene, and he can't tell me when we will be able to go back to work."

I stared, wide-eyed. "A *crime* scene? Because Blake fell in the moat? What, is stupidity a crime now?"

Barry shook his head. "Maybe it ought to be, but it isn't." He took a deep breath and said softly, "But murder is."

When my mug hit the concrete floor it shattered into little pieces. Hot coffee sprayed across the floor and onto the fronts of the storage cabinets.

No. It had to be a mistake.

"But, he drowned! I saw him!"

Barry bent down and began picking up the pieces of the shattered mug. Paula appeared in the doorway, looking worried. "Are you okay?" she asked.

I wanted to shout that I wasn't okay, that I wouldn't be okay, that okay was out of the question for the foreseeable future. "Sure," I said. "Just dropped my cup. Sorry, I'll get you another one."

Paula crossed the room in two quick steps and wrapped an arm around my shoulders. "Don't worry about the cup, Georgie. I just want to be sure you are all right."

"Yeah, I'll be fine," I lied. "But I better give Barry a hand cleaning up my mess. He has rules about leaving a mess, you know."

Paula smiled at my feeble joke. "They're his rules, he can deal with them."

"No, I need to help him. Thanks."

I stepped out of the comfort of her arm, grabbed a rag from under the sink, and started wiping up the cabinets. Paula nodded and went back to her desk.

Barry and I quickly mopped up the coffee and tossed the broken cup in the trash. When we were done, he poured me another cup. He pulled a chair in from the main room of the library, and sat me down before handing me the coffee.

"I just came from the sheriff's office. He has the Medical Examiner's report, and Mr. Weston did not drown. He was hit in the midsection, hard enough to break ribs and cause other damage. They aren't saying what hit him, but they *are* sure it wasn't an accident. They're searching the job site for possible weapons."

It was a good thing I was sitting down, because I didn't think my legs would hold me. My stomach churned with the acid of the coffee, and a cold chill ran through me. I'd accepted Blake's death, or so I thought.

But the idea that he was murdered was too much.

It took a couple minutes for the adrenaline surge to pass. That's when I started shaking. When I left San Francisco I hated Blake. Just a few days ago I was wishing I would never see him again.

But those emotions, as intense as they were, didn't mean I wished he was dead. But he was. And someone had been angry enough to kill him.

The tremors subsided. Barry stood by me, waiting and watching, in case I needed him. But I drew a few deep, calming breaths, letting go of my inner turmoil.

"Do you want to rest here awhile, Georgie? Paula says you're welcome to stay."

I suddenly remembered the trunk full of groceries. Even if I was still employed, they represented a significant percentage of my bank account. I needed to get them in the refrigerator.

"I — I need to get home. The groceries . . ." My voice trailed off, but Barry knew what I was talking about.

"You want me to drive you?" he offered.

I stood up carefully, and waved him away. It was sweet of him, but I just wanted to be alone and try to process the fact that Blake had been murdered.

"I'm okay, Barry. It's a shock, but I'll be fine."

I tried a smile that felt like it didn't fit my face, and took a few steps toward the front door. My legs held me up, although I felt as though my head was a helium balloon, floating above my body.

I made my way to the door, waving to Paula as I went by.

"I'll talk to you later," I said without stopping.

I don't remember the drive home, or what I did once I arrived. But later the car was in the driveway and the groceries were put away. I must have managed somehow.

CHAPTER 17

The phone rang constantly all afternoon. News travels fast in a small town, and by now everyone would know that Blake was murdered. Most of them already knew that I had known him.

I ignored it.

Finally, late in the day, someone knocked on the door. I peeked out the kitchen window, and caught a glimpse of Wade's hybrid sedan in the driveway.

Even knowing it was Wade, I hesitated. But he was one of the people I was learning to trust, wasn't he?

I opened the door and let him in.

As soon as the door was safely closed and locked behind him, Wade pulled me into his arms and gave me a comforting hug.

"I know you said he was just someone you used to work with, Georgie. But Paula called me after you left the library. She said you were upset by the news." He drew back and looked down at me. "I've been trying to call you all day."

I glanced guiltily toward the answering machine. Messages had been stacking up all day from people I didn't want to talk to. But that shouldn't have included Wade.

"I'm sorry, Wade. I didn't want to talk to anyone after Barry told me. It sounded so horrible, and it happened right where I was working."

Wade drew me over to the sofa, and sat down beside me. "It was just a coincidence. He wasn't out there looking for you."

"Not at that hour. I mean, he knew I would be there, knew I was working the site."

Wade tilted my chin up so that I was looking him in the eye. "The guy came to Pine Ridge on a job. It had nothing to do with you. If you hadn't talked to him since you left San Francisco, he didn't even know you were here when he arrived.

"Whoever killed him — it wasn't your fault."

I shook my head. "I suppose you're right, Wade. It was just a shock."

I looked away and took a deep breath. They say confession is good for the soul, and my soul needed all the soothing it could get right then.

"We were more than coworkers, Wade. We were business partners, and we dated — seriously — for several months. Well, at least I was serious. Him, I'm not so sure.

"It all crashed and burned, almost overnight. One day I was running my company with the guidance of the board of directors and dating my partner. The next day I'd been dumped, and I was out of a job."

I glanced up at him and quickly looked away. I would have to face his reaction, but not this instant.

"Until this week, no one in Pine Ridge knew anything about San Francisco. Until I talked to Sue last night, no one knew the whole story.

"And now you."

I hadn't given him all the gory details, but he knew enough. And I was sure he could fill in the rest.

Wade sat quiet for a moment, while I struggled to control my swirling emotions. This was far worse than his covering for his buddy in high school, and I'd broken up with him over that.

Even dead, Blake was still screwing up my life.

"Did you still have feelings for him, Georgie?"

I shrugged. "I suppose. If you call hating

181

his guts feelings."

Wade chuckled, and I risked a quick look.

His face was serious, but his eyes were warm and full of concern. He didn't look like a guy who was about to dump me.

"Are you hungry?"

Huh? Was everyone getting on the Sue Gibbons conversation roller coaster? Who thought about food at a time like this?

Wade, apparently. He took my silence as agreement and stood up.

But instead of helping me up, he reached for the afghan on the back of the sofa and spread it over my legs.

"Sit there," he directed. "I'm going to feed the dogs and make us some dinner. All you have to do right now is stay where you are, and let me take care of you."

I started to protest, and he held up a hand. "No arguments, Neverall. I know you can take care of yourself — even when people are shooting at you — but sometimes you have to let other people fuss over you.

"This is one of those times."

He crouched down so that he was at eye level with me. "This was a shock for all of us. We all feel it. But you knew him, pretty well it sounds like, and it's got to hit you a lot harder. Just take some time, okay?"

I nodded. The fight had gone out of me

when Barry told me Blake was murdered. It was easier to just sit back, pull the afghan up to my chin, and nod.

Wade hurried into the kitchen, as though he was afraid I would change my mind. We both knew my attitude would change soon, and Wade was determined to take advantage of it while it lasted. It wasn't often that I let him fuss.

I listened to the racket from the kitchen for a few minutes before I got up and went in to check on him.

"Back to your couch," Wade ordered. But there was a laugh in his tone. "I knew you wouldn't last."

"It sounded like you could use some help finding things."

Wade looked around at my bare-bones assemblage of tools and equipment. "I could. If you had the things I'm looking for." He rummaged through the drawer next to the stove. "How do you function without a ladle?"

"I'm one person. What do I need a ladle for?"

Wade rolled his eyes at me. "You can just toddle back to the sofa, lady without a ladle. Turn on the TV, or watch a movie or something. Dinner will be ready soon."

I took the hint and went back to the living

room. But I couldn't settle down, and found myself scanning the shelf of DVDs next to the television. I pulled down several cases, looking for a movie equivalent of comfort food.

In a few minutes, Wade started ferrying food from the kitchen to the living room.

"This would be a lot easier if you had a tray," he said on the third trip.

There were already two bowls of chicken noodle soup on the trunk, and the dogs had come sniffing in, looking hopeful. I gave them a stern look and they retreated to their beds with a big doggy sigh.

They looked up when Wade came in again. He was carrying a plate piled with diagonal cut grilled-cheese sandwiches. Little bits of orangey melted cheese oozed out the sides and dripped onto the plate.

I shook my head at the dogs, and they put their heads down. They knew there was no chance they were getting our dinner.

Wade handed me a plate with a bowl of soup and a piece of cheese sandwich. He spread a napkin over my lap. "Chicken noodle and grilled cheese. The ultimate comfort food dinner."

He gave me a sheepish grin. "Well, the ultimate dinner I can cook. I suppose there are others."

He sat down next to me, and glanced at the TV. Frozen on the screen were the opening credits of *Real Genius*.

He looked back at me. "A little nostalgia?"

I nodded. "I suppose. All I know is that it makes me feel better."

Wade took his own plate and sat back, propping his feet up.

I pushed "Play" and spooned up my soup. By the time Val Kilmer's Chris Knight was explaining the temporary ice to sycophant Kent, I had finished my soup and sandwich and was reaching for another half.

I'd seen the movie dozens of times — it was an unofficial Caltech orientation — and I found myself mouthing punch lines along with the characters. I smiled when my on-screen alter ego — Jordan — got the guy, and giggled in anticipation before the first kernel of popcorn popped in the final act.

The credits rolled as Tears For Fears sang about everybody wanting to rule the world. I let it run. I didn't want the movie to end, because I'd have to come back to reality.

"Was it really like that?" Wade asked when the last name had scrolled past and the studio logo filled the screen.

"Pretty much," I replied. "I never got invited to a pool party in a lecture hall, but otherwise it wasn't far off. The pressure?

That was completely real.

"Like when the guy in the study scene stands up and just starts screaming? We all had days like that. Every year there were a couple people who couldn't take it. Usually they would go home for a holiday or something and just not come back."

I sat for a minute lost in the memories of my years at one of the country's toughest schools. "There was this one time, after finals?"

Wade nodded. "That meant keggers at my school."

"I'm sure there were those, too. But this time we had just finished finals, and I walked into one of the lounges. There was a girl sitting at a table with a little kid's coloring book and a great big box of crayons. You know the kind with sixty-four colors and a sharpener built into the box?"

"A coloring book?"

"Yeah. She looked up at me, and said in this little girl voice, 'I am coloring because I can.' It was that kind of place."

"And yet you stayed. Why not pack it in and come back here to go to school?"

I took the last piece of sandwich off the plate. I held it up to Wade with a questioning look and he shook his head. "If you're sure," I said, and took a bite. Even stone

186

cold it was still good. It was hard to mess up grilled cheese.

I thought about Wade's question as I chewed the cold sandwich. Why had I stayed in the pressure cooker that was Tech? Why had I worked so hard to finish my degree, and then turned around and gone right to work on my Masters?

"I couldn't imagine *not* doing it," I said finally.

Wade chuckled softly. "And you were too stubborn to quit — too proud to give up."

I laughed, too. "Maybe so. But I truly loved what I was doing. I was learning about things that interested me, studying stuff I wanted to know. There wasn't anywhere I would have rather been."

"The computers or the math?"

I scowled. "What do you know about that?"

He gave me a sheepish grin. "I talked to your dad a couple times after you first went away. He told me a lot about what you were doing, and bragged about how well you were getting along. He was really proud of you."

"I'm glad of that." I swallowed the lump in my throat and moved back to relatively safer ground. "I liked it all, I think. The math was interesting, but it was mostly a means to an end; a way to understand the computer better. The field was moving faster and faster, changing so rapidly it seemed like the minute you learned something it was out of date. But that was part of what I loved about it."

Wade got up and took the DVD out of the player and returned it to its case. He put the case on the shelf, picked up the dirty dishes, and carried them to the kitchen.

"Then why did you quit, Georgie?"

"I told you, I lost my job."

Wade came back from the kitchen. He looked like he wanted to say something more, but he seemed to think better of it. Instead he settled back onto the sofa and put his arm across my shoulders.

"You getting tired yet?" he asked.

I yawned and stretched. "Yeah, a bit."

He stood up and offered me his hand. He pulled me up out of the sofa and laid the afghan over the back. "Go to bed. I'll finish cleaning up here."

I'd spent all evening taking orders from Wade. For tonight only, it was a habit. I went to bed.

CHAPTER 18

The smell of coffee woke me up. There shouldn't be coffee. Not unless the dogs had developed opposable thumbs overnight. And even if they had, they would use them for something more to their liking than coffee. Maybe getting their own green treats from the cupboard.

The fog lifted a little from my brain. Blake's death. Murder. Wade making dinner.

Wade. I remember him promising to clean up if I went to bed. What I didn't remember was him leaving. I had not asked him to stay, but my nose was telling me he did.

I put on my robe — the heavy quilted one that zipped all the way to my chin. I stopped in the bathroom to run a comb through my hair and splash water on my face.

In the kitchen Wade had a big pot of coffee, and a goofy grin. "I slept on the couch," he said. The wrinkles in his clothes and his bed-head hair testified to that.

"You'd had a rough day. I figured you might have a bad night. Are you feeling any better this morning?"

I took the cup of coffee he offered me, and leaned against the counter. "I'm okay, I guess."

I looked around for the dogs.

"I let them out a few minutes ago," Wade said. "The phone's been ringing for a couple hours. I turned the ringer off so it wouldn't wake you."

"Thanks." I looked over at the answering machine. It blinked steadily, and the message counter was in double digits. "I've been ignoring the messages, but I'll have to deal with them pretty soon."

"Yeah. Some guy named Stan called a couple times already this morning. Seemed to be anxious to talk to you."

Stan. I had forgotten about him last night, but escape time was over. It was time for the real world again.

"Uh, Wade, about last night?"

"Yeah?"

"You know all the things I told you? They're not things I want to share with the world. It's kind of embarrassing to have people know I got thrown out of my own company. And it's humiliating to have everyone know I got dumped."

He looked me in the eye. "Yes, that it is."

I felt a hot flush creeping up my neck and across my face. Wade knew exactly how humiliating it was, and I was the reason.

"Oh, Wade, I'm sorry!"

He shrugged. "Long time ago."

He walked to the back door and took a look out to check on the dogs before he continued. "But you don't need to worry. I know how to keep a secret. Remember, my job gives me access to the finances of half the people in this town. I keep the books for their businesses, do their taxes, help them with college aid applications, set up retirement accounts — just about any kind of financial advice or service they need. If I can't keep things confidential, I'm out of business."

"I know." I felt bad for even bringing it up and it showed clearly in my tone.

"Your secrets are safe with me." Wade raised three fingers in a scout salute and made a solemn face.

It was a serious promise, but I had to chuckle at his clowning around. He grinned back and glanced up at the clock on the kitchen wall.

"If you're okay," he said, his voice serious once again, "I really should take off. Before someone calls your mother and reports that my car was here all night."

I rolled my eyes. "Probably too late, Councilman Montgomery. I'd be willing to bet your reputation is already in tatters. And all for nothing, I'm afraid."

He recoiled in mock horror. "I am shocked. Shocked, I tell you! A respected City Councilman!"

He chuckled. "You don't think people would approve of my spending the night with the best-looking plumber in town?"

Considering my dowdy bathrobe and general early-morning dishevelment, it seemed like a huge compliment. "Gee, thanks, Wade," I said with a touch of sarcasm. "Since I'm the only female plumber in town, I suppose that's a good thing."

He grinned at me, then his expression grew serious again. "Are you sure you're okay? I can stay if you need me."

I shook my head. "Get out of here. You have better things to do than hang around and wait on me."

I headed to the living room, and he followed.

"If you're sure . . ."

"Wade, I really appreciate what you did. The last couple days have been incredibly stressful, and you gave me a chance to relax for a few hours. I'm much better this morning — a night's sleep will do that for you — and you need to get home."

I took his jacket off the hook near the front door. "Thank you. It was exactly what I needed."

Wade shrugged into his jacket. He reached over and put his hands on my shoulders. "Anytime, Georgie. Call me if you need me." He bent down and kissed my forehead. "Okay?"

"Sure, Wade. And thanks again."

He started down the front steps, then turned back. "Don't forget the dogs are outside."

The dogs got their treats, and I was pouring a second cup of coffee when the answering machine picked up again. The volume was turned low, and at first I ignored it, just as I had for the last couple days.

When I heard Stan Fischer's booming voice, though, I picked up. He'd been part of the board that ousted me, but Stan had been the one person who offered me a chance to get out of Samurai with some shred of dignity.

"Hi, Stan. It's Georgiana. How are you?"

"Georgie Girl! Good to hear your voice! Wondered what had happened to you after you left S.F. I thought you might keep in touch, but nobody ever heard from you." His voice dropped into a somber register and he went on. "Terrible thing about Blake. Terrible. When they first called me I thought it was an accident, but now the sheriff says he was murdered. Have you heard anything about that, Georgie Girl?"

I cringed every time he used that name, but there was nothing I could do. He thought it was cute and told me I should take it as a compliment. Why, I wasn't sure, but I had learned there were some things that weren't worth arguing about with Stan Fischer.

"To tell the truth, Stan, I was going to ask you the same question. I only just heard they were calling it a murder." There wasn't anything I could add.

"I'm supposed to come out there and talk to the sheriff this morning," Stan replied, "but I'd like a chance to see you before I do. You know, get the skinny on what the place is really like, maybe figure out what Blake was doing."

"I'd love to see you," I answered. I didn't have to even think about it. There was still a soft spot for Stan Fischer in spite of all that had happened.

"How about you let an old man buy you breakfast? Anywhere in that burg serve a

194

decent one?"

I laughed, remembering Stan's definition of a decent breakfast. Although he hadn't worked on the pipeline in decades, he retained an addiction to caffeine, salt, and grease.

Dee's would be perfect.

"Breakfast sounds fine, Stan. And it would be great to see you, but who's this old man you're bringing along?"

I paused to listen to his answering guffaw. "And is there any reason this should be a private meeting?" I asked. It was the phrase he had used with me, the day he offered me the chance to resign.

"None I can think of," he answered. "Can you?"

There were dozens, starting with not publicizing my connection with Samurai and the late Blake Weston. Dee's was tiny, but it was gossip central for Pine Ridge.

Too bad. Everyone was going to know soon enough, if they didn't already. Now that Blake's death had been ruled a murder, it would be the single biggest topic of conversation in town.

All I could hope for was damage control. And talking to Stan Fischer was the first step in that process.

"Not a one," I lied. "There's a place here

in town that's exactly what you like."

We spent a few minutes planning to meet at Dee's. I started to give him directions, but he dismissed them. "Got a GPS in the rental car," he said. "I'll be able to find it, no problem."

I figured the time it would take Stan to drive out from his hotel. Traffic shouldn't be as bad on Saturday, but I didn't want to be late. Still, there was time enough to take a shower and make myself presentable.

I slid into the next-to-last booth at Dee's twenty-five minutes later. A couple other booths were occupied, but not by anyone I knew well. I'd grabbed a mug of coffee on my way past the counter, and told Dee a friend of mind would be along in a few minutes and we'd order when he got there.

I picked up the local weekly, abandoned by an earlier customer on the end of the counter.

A report on a zoning dispute filled the front page, spilling over onto page four. It was a sign of things to come. Another project like McComb's would never get approval.

I read the end of the article and glanced at a couple others. Typical small-town reporting: a local high school girl had been selected as an exchange student and was raising money to fund her trip; the grammar school would be closed on Thursday and Friday for parent conferences; a picture of Janis Breckweth handing an oversized check to Carl from Homes for Hope. Martha Tepper's estate had been settled, and the check represented her bequest to the building fund.

I flipped back to page one and scanned the rest of the week's front-page stories. Blake's death was a small box at the bottom of the page. He was identified as an out-of-town consultant for new residents Chad and Astrid McComb, and the article said the investigation into his death was ongoing.

Nothing I didn't already know.

The *new residents* line did amuse me. Chad and Astrid had been working on the moat project for many months, and had pumped a lot of money into the local economy. They were well liked, and they treated everyone with respect. But until they had survived a couple winters in the relative isolation of a small town at the foot of a large mountain, they would remain "new" residents. Too many people before them had fled back to the city; they had to prove themselves to the locals.

I looked up from the paper in time to see Stan Fischer come through the front door of Dee's. He wore an expensive raincoat and hat I was sure cost more than I made in a week, and yet he looked completely at home in the tiny diner.

I guessed wife number four — or was it five? I'd lost count a few years back, and there could have been more since I left — had tried to make him over, but the oil field roughneck still lived just below the spiffed-up exterior.

It was reassuring to know that some things never change.

Stan spotted me, and a wide smile spread across his broad face. As he walked back to where I sat, I stood up and greeted him with a hug.

"Stan! It's good to see you."

"You, too, Georgie. You, too."

We took a moment to scan the chalkboard behind the counter that held today's menu and then stepped to the counter to give Dee our orders. Stan wanted the works: eggs, bacon, home fries, toast, and a side of pancakes.

When we sat back down, he frowned slightly. "A sad business, this thing with Blake," he said. "It's really good to see you again, but I'd hoped it would be under better circumstances."

I nodded. "Yeah. I'm sorry about Blake.

He was really good at what he did. I'm sure it's a huge loss for you."

"For all of us," Stan replied. He sipped his coffee before adding a large amount of cream, and several packets of sugar.

"I was excited when he told me he'd found you, Georgie. And so was he. Said he was going to have a talk with you."

"About what? I saw him a couple times, but it seemed like all he wanted to do was make snide comments."

"He was a little defensive, I guess. Thought you wouldn't want to talk to him after what he did. But I urged him to speak to you, to give you a chance to, I don't know, maybe put the past behind you."

"I've put the past behind me, Stan, in case you hadn't noticed. I moved almost a thousand miles away," I exaggerated, "and I started a new career. Something that has nothing to do with computers, or security."

"And how's that workin' for you?"

"Just fine."

Stan gave me a look that said he didn't believe a word I said. He chewed his eggs and toast, and washed it down with a big gulp of sweet coffee before he prodded me.

"You sure about that?"

"I walked away, Stan. That's what mattered. I jumped. I wasn't pushed. And it didn't take Blake Weston to make me know I made the right decision."

I was being defensive, but Stan was poking at scar tissue, and I wanted him to leave it alone.

"Georgie" — he put down his fork and reached across to pat my hand — "do you mean to tell me you and Blake did not have a conversation about you coming back to Samurai?"

All I could do was stare. There was no way Blake would have asked me to come back to Samurai, and there was absolutely no way I would have agreed.

The whole idea was ridiculous.

"What do you mean, come back to Samurai?"

CHAPTER 19

"Just what I said. Blake said he was thinking we ought to ask you to come back to Samurai."

I took a bite of waffle. It tasted like sawdust, and I couldn't swallow.

"You know the industry, Georgie. Like sharks. Move or die. We have to keep moving, keep innovating, to stay competitive."

He picked up his fork and shoved a pile of hash browns into his mouth. When he finished chewing, he took another big gulp of coffee. "Blake said, and this is a direct quote, 'No matter what happened with me and Georgiana, she was the most innovative thinker we had. We were foolish to let her go.' "

I picked up my coffee and took a drink, forcing the clump of waffle down my throat. Blake had wanted me to come back? *Blake?* The man who had tried to provoke me into a fight in front of the entire crew at Mc-

Comb's? The guy who sneered at me in Tiny's, when Chad told him I was working with the plumbing crew?

That Blake?

It made no sense.

"He didn't mean that."

"He most certainly did. Told me so himself when he called from up here, the night before he died. Said he was going to talk to you, that Samurai needed you, and he had to put the best interests of the company ahead of his personal concerns."

Stan shook his head. "I tried to tell you, office romances never work out."

Yes, Stan had tried to tell us exactly that when he arrived, but since Blake and I were already partners — personally and professionally — we had chosen not to heed his advice.

I struggled to hold back a laugh, knowing the source of his wisdom. It seemed that several of the former Mrs. Fischers had come from exactly that origin. Of course he didn't believe in romance in the workplace. It had worked so well for him, after all.

"Well, he may have talked to you, Stan, but the man didn't say a thing to me about Samurai. In fact, all he said was that he was here on a job for McComb. I don't think he even mentioned Samurai directly. To tell the truth, I wondered if he was still working for you."

"He was — one of our best. And this Mc-Comb deal was important enough to deserve our best. A chance to expand, maybe even open a Northwest office. Something we've talked about for a long time."

I remembered the heady days when the customer demand was growing faster than the business. We were running full speed just to keep up. We had dreamed of expanding beyond the Bay Area. The Northwest was the natural first step, but we hadn't moved in that direction before I left.

"My problem now is, I don't have anyone I can put into Blake's spot here. We're stretched thin when it comes to the really talented people. Just like we always were."

He signaled Dee with his coffee mug, and she shuffled over with a refill. "How was your breakfast?" she asked as she poured.

"Before I answer that, will you answer a question for me?"

Dee furrowed her brow and gave him a stern look.

"One question?" Stan wheedled. He was a flirt, though he wasn't very good at it. When you have his kind of money, you don't have to be.

Dee waited stoically, the coffee pot in her hand.

"I think I'm in love. Are you married?"

I had never in my life seen Dee blush. A rosy color crept over her cheeks and down her neck. She didn't answer Stan, just waved dismissively, and walked away.

"This is the best meal I've had in years," he said. He looked down at his plate where a faint trace of egg yolk tinted the white surface a pale yellow, then back up at me. "And I don't want to hear a word about calories or cholesterol or any of the rest of it." He snorted. "The soon-to-be ex-Mrs. Fischer thought she needed to reform my eating habits."

I wondered if this was the same Mrs. Fischer I had met. She had been a waitress before she retired to spend Stan's money. She'd probably get a tidy settlement, as the others had, before he went looking for his next victim, er, spouse.

Stan had that look in his eye — the one that said he was hatching a scheme that was going to make a lot of work for everyone involved. That usually meant a lot of work for him, too. And a tidy profit.

It was a look that sent a shiver of anticipation through me. When Stan got that look, anything could happen.

"If Blake had asked, about coming back to Samurai, what would you have said?"

I stared in disbelief. "You are kidding, right? You know what I would have said. Not just no, but . . ."

Stan chuckled. "Are you sure?"

"I'm sure, Stan. I was through with Blake, through with Samurai, through with the whole industry.

"Blake could have stood by me against the board, and we might have been able to convince them we were right. But he saw which way the political winds were blowing and he made his choice."

"Then what if *I* asked you?"

"You wouldn't," I answered without hesitation. "You still have to work with the board, and they wanted me out. I don't think Blake would have done it, either."

"Then would you consider acting as a consultant for me? Just this one job. The board won't even have to know. I'll tell them I hired a local hotshot who was able to step in." He took a last sip of coffee. "That much would be the truth."

"You mean the McComb job?"

"Exactly! Blake was the best we had, but you were better, and we both know it. The hourly rate should be attractive, you don't have to leave home, and you are already

205

familiar with the site. Everybody wins."

For one insane instant I considered the offer. I could use the money, and as long as the board didn't have to know who the "local hotshot" was I might be able to get away with it.

Except that this was a specialized field. Innovation had moved at lightning speed when I was up-to-date on the latest developments. There was no way I could hope to do the job Blake had been sent here to do.

"I'm flattered, Stan. I really am. But it just wouldn't work. I'm out of the loop — haven't kept up with the field in a couple years. Everything I know is out of date, and there isn't time for me to catch up — even if I wanted to.

"You know that."

Stan smiled a little sadly. "Yeah, that's kind of what I expected you to say. But you can't blame a guy for trying, especially when I'd really like to have you back on the team."

I smiled back. "Thanks." He had his wallet out, and dropped a handful of bills on the table. "And thanks for the breakfast."

"Thanks for the recommendation. Exactly what I wanted."

We stood up and Stan followed me to the sidewalk. There was no question which car was his. The Lincoln Town Car stood out on a street full of pickups.

Stan looked at the neighboring trucks. "You get rid of the car, too?" he asked.

I shook my head. "Keep it garaged. A convertible doesn't make a lot of sense in the rainy season." I didn't bother to explain that rainy season included most of the year.

"Good. You deserved that car." He clicked a remote and the Lincoln flashed its lights. Another click and the engine purred to life.

"Where's the sheriff's office?" Stan asked. "I have to stop and talk to him before I go see the McCombs. I wish I knew what I was going to tell them."

I pointed to the corner. "Two blocks to the right."

He opened the car door, climbed in and opened the passenger's window. He leaned across the seat. "Thanks, Georgie. I hope we can get together again before I have to go home. This shouldn't take too long, but the board wants me to report back to them as soon as possible."

"That'd be great.

"As for the McCombs, tell them you have some good people back in San Francisco, and you will get one of them up here just as soon as you can. I'm sure you have someone down there that can do the job.

"They're reasonable people, I'm sure

they'll understand."

Stan waved as he closed the window and pulled away from the curb.

I knew he had Richard Parks, who was at least as capable as I was. More so, now that I wasn't keeping up with the world of high-tech security. But I had promised Richard I wouldn't tell Stan he'd called.

Somehow I had never had the chance to ask him about the rumor that I'd taken a buyout. There hadn't been a way to work it into the conversation without revealing where I'd heard it.

Maybe he hadn't even heard the rumor, though I doubted it. If it weren't for his rough edges, Stan would have been more than a match for Blake in the office politics department. Even with the rough edges he managed to keep on top of most of what went on around Samurai Security.

I'd just have to find a way to ask him the next time I saw him. And I had to make sure there was a next time.

CHAPTER 20

I stood on the sidewalk a moment longer, looking at the corner where Stan's rented Lincoln had disappeared. I was amazed at how happy I had been to see him, and how angry I had been to see Blake.

Well, duh! One had treated me kindly, offered me the opportunity to salvage a little dignity, and been pleased to see me.

The other had dumped me with a voice mail, humiliated me in public, and apparently spread some nasty lies about my departure from Samurai.

The voice mail hurt, but the lies made me angry. Richard, and by extension the rest of the company, thought I waltzed out the door with a pot of money. They were more likely to think of me as the owner of the castle, not the ditchdigger.

I left the Beetle at the curb and walked down the street to Doggy Day Spa. My conversation with Stan was too weird not to share with somebody, and I trusted Sue.

When I opened the door, I was greeted with a chorus of barking from the kennels at the back. Sue was at the grooming table with a sheepdog puppy, and his brother was in the kennel, complaining loudly about the separation.

Astrid McComb stood next to Sue, absorbed in watching her comb out the sheepdog's coat.

Sue did that a lot with her clients, instructing them in the proper care of their dogs. Sometimes it cut down on the trips to the groomer, but she said it mostly cut down on the complaints about her fees.

"When they know how much work it really is to bathe and clip and groom their dog, they figure they're getting a bargain."

Compared to the fees I'd paid in San Francisco, they definitely were.

Sue patiently combed and clipped, all the while talking soothingly to the puppy. I waited to one side, unwilling to interrupt the lesson.

Astrid took the comb from Sue, and timidly ran it over a section of the sheepdog's coat. Sue encouraged her, and she was soon combing and crooning, just as Sue had done.

Sue left Astrid with the puppy and walked

up front to where I waited. "She adores those puppies, but she's a little intimidated by their care." She looked at Astrid and back at me. "She'll be fine. Just needs a little encouragement and some practice."

"You're good with the dogs *and* the owners."

"What are you doing here? Two visits in the same week without the dogs is a bad sign, Georgie."

"Subtle much, Gibbons?" I shook my head. "I just had breakfast with Stan Fischer — the guy from San Francisco I told you about — and I don't know what to think."

"You mean like is he one of the bad guys? I heard the sheriff is saying it wasn't an accident."

"No, I don't think he's one of the bad guys. I told you, he was the one person who was good to me when I left San Francisco." I glanced up to be sure Astrid was still busy with her puppy. "It was something else. Something I don't want to talk about in front of anyone."

Sue took the hint. "I'll be through here in a few minutes. Why don't you go back and take a look at the computer? I would appreciate it if you would check that the backups are working right since you fixed it the other day."

I retreated to Sue's office and logged on to her computer. I poked around in the system, checking that her firewalls were intact and her virus protection was updating correctly.

I pulled out her backups and checked that they were working properly. I did everything except what I really wanted to do: get on the Internet and see what I could find out about the current status of Samurai Security.

It seemed odd that I had not done an online search before now, but I had tried to put it all in the past. Checking up on the company would only reopen the wounds. Checking up on Blake bordered on stalker behavior. I'd managed to avoid both.

But now the temptation was nearly overwhelming. There might be a clue to Blake's murder. The sheriff might not recognize it since he didn't know the people involved like I did. It would be a way I could help with the investigation.

Justification much, Neverall? If I wanted an excuse to Google Samurai Security, Stan's offer should be adequate. But I had turned down his proposal, so there was no reason to look. Was there?

Wade's question from the previous night rattled around my brain. Why had I left high tech?

I could go on forever about the dreadful working conditions, the long hours, the complete immersion in work to the detriment of everything else in my life. I could talk about the whirlwind pace, the exhaustion, the meals eaten at my desk or around a conference table in the middle of the night.

But was that really the reason? Maybe it was the realization that Richard Parks — or someone like him — could do my job in a heartbeat and do it better. I was no longer the hot young thing, out to set the computing world on fire.

Maybe that was what Blake had fallen for; the top dog who led the pack. And when he saw that position slipping he didn't care about what was left.

I dismissed that opportunity to wallow in self-pity.

I'd told Wade I loved what I was doing, and it was true. I still enjoyed messing with Sue's computer, and Barry's. It felt good to solve a problem, to make the machines run faster and smoother, to protect them from worms and viruses.

That was one of my favorite parts, actually. The feeling that I had defeated some bozo whose idea of fun was to damage or destroy the computers and data of complete strangers.

It was even better when we were able to trace the source of the infection and find the person responsible. Sometimes it was just a kid with the electronic equivalent of a can of spray paint. But sometimes it was more than that.

Was that why Stan's offer had tempted me? The chance to beat the vandals out there?

Or was it that I wanted to prove I still had what it takes, to prove to myself and the board of Samurai Security that they had made a mistake when they booted me out?

Maybe my decisions weren't as much in the past as I wanted them to be.

I was resisting the urge to just poke around a little when Sue came back to the office.

"Coast's clear," she said, sticking her head around the door frame. "But I need to stay up front. Come on up when you're through."

"I'm through," I said, pushing aside the temptation and standing up.

I followed Sue to the front of the shop. Astrid and the sheepdogs were gone.

Sue set to work cleaning and disinfecting the grooming table, sink, and floor. "I've got a standard poodle coming this afternoon. You don't mind if I keep working while we talk, do you?"

"Since I barged in on you in the middle of your workday I really can't complain about you actually working, can I?"

"Suppose not," Sue answered as she sprayed the grooming table with a plastic bottle. "So what was so important that you barged in — as you put it — in the middle of the workday?"

"I had breakfast with Stan, like I told you."

"And Astrid couldn't overhear that? I think perhaps you're getting a little too invested in the whole keeping-secrets thing."

The disinfectant stung my nose and I sneezed.

"Bless you."

"Thanks. That stuff stinks."

"But it stinks in a clean way. The customers like to know the place is clean when they bring in their pets.

"And don't try to change the subject."

I rolled my eyes. Miss Roller Coaster Conversationalist telling *me* not to change the subject.

"I mean it," Sue said. "You still haven't told me why we had to wait until Astrid was gone."

"I wasn't sure she'd be very happy with

the idea of a member of her plumbing crew being offered the chance to design her new security system."

"Are you serious?" Sue dropped her cleaning rag and grabbed me in a bear hug. "That is sooo cool! You're really good at that stuff, and I bet McComb's paying big money for the new system." She retreated to her cleaning again. "And who isn't in favor of big money?"

She turned and looked at me. "No wonder you think this Stan is one of the good guys."

"I turned him down."

"You did *what?*"

"I turned him down. There's no way I can do the job, Sue. I'm totally out of touch."

"But you take care of my computer, and Barry's. And you have all that equipment set up in your house. You know this stuff, Georgie. How could you say no?"

"Because I don't know that much, not really. Not at the level the McCombs would need. Think about what they do. They worked at the leading edge of the industry for a lot of years. Their computers are going to be light-years ahead of yours and Barry's. And me . . ." I shook my head. "No. there's no way I could do that job."

Sue straightened up from sweeping hair into a dustpan. "No one said you had to do the job." She emptied the dustpan. "Just take it."

I wondered if I looked as puzzled as I felt.

Apparently so. Sue put her hands on her hips. "After the way they treated you? Why shouldn't you just take the money, do what you can, and leave the rest for them to finish?"

"That's the most ridiculous idea you've had yet."

"Is it? What do you owe these people? They took your company, they treated you like dirt, and now they want you to pick up the pieces when their hotshot consultant gets himself killed?" She slammed her hand down on the grooming table. "Nothing, Georgie. That's what you owe them!"

"I didn't say I owed them anything. But Stan told me some stuff that makes me wonder."

"Like what?" she challenged.

"Like Blake told him he wanted to ask me to come back to Samurai, that they needed me. That what happened between us didn't matter as much as the future of the company."

She snorted. "He should have thought of that before he left you that voice mail."

"But here's what doesn't make sense, Sue. Why was he killed up here? What was he doing that made him a target?"

"If his history is any indication, he was probably being a total jerk. But I don't think that's what you meant. Besides, how do you know it had anything to do with what he was doing here? Maybe somebody followed him or something."

"And they just happened to be out at the McComb site?

"No. I've been thinking about this ever since I heard. Something changed. He made somebody angry, or he got in someone's way."

Something niggled in the back of my head. "There was one person," I said. "Someone who asked an awful lot of questions about Blake and what he was doing here."

"There was? Who?"

"Gregory Whitlock —"

"Not this again! You don't like the man, which I totally understand, so every time something bad happens you want to make him responsible."

"This is different. I mean, yeah, I suspected him when Martha Tepper disappeared, but I only thought he was trying to make money by cheating her. I never thought he killed her."

Sue shook her head. "You were ready and

willing to believe he was responsible for everything that happened."

"Not really," I argued. "Not once we knew she was dead."

"So if he wasn't a murderer then, what makes him one now?"

"I didn't say he was a murderer. I said he asked a lot of questions about Blake. Sue, he practically gives me the third degree every time I see him.

"It's creepy."

"Because he is your mother's boyfriend."

"Not because he's my mother's boy-friend." I leaned over the grooming table, putting my face close to hers. "Because he kept asking questions about the guy, and then he ends up dead."

Sue threw her hands in the air. "So he was asking questions? So what?"

"It just seemed like —" I sputtered to a stop. Maybe she was right. Maybe I wasn't being fair to Gregory. Yeah, and maybe mon-keys . . .

"Okay, whatever. But, Sue, his questions were creepy. He kept asking about things I really didn't know, and trying to make something out of the argument at Mc-Combs's; like I was doing something wrong."

"You mean like screaming at the guy in

front of the entire crew? Like that?"

I made a face. "You think that wasn't such a good thing to do?" I asked sheepishly. I hate it when she's right.

"Not good, no. You know the sheriff's going to be wanting to talk to you again, now that he knows it wasn't an accident."

I bit back an expletive. Barry's training was taking over even off the job. "I hadn't thought of it that way. You don't really think he'd suspect me, do you?"

Sue refused to look at me.

"Does he *already* suspect me?"

"I don't know." Her voice was low, her tone miserable. "I know he's upset that your friend — former friend, ex-partner, whatever — was murdered here in Pine Ridge."

She finally looked at me, her eyes begging for understanding. "He takes the safety and security of this town very seriously, Georgie. He just wants to find whoever did it and lock them up."

"Even if it's me?"

"If you'd done it, of course! I don't think he really believes you'd do such a thing. But it wouldn't matter who it was — even Gregory Whitlock with all his money and influence."

I shook my head. It didn't make me happy, but I knew it was the truth. "I'm sorry. That was a dumb question."

"Sure was."

"I don't think I'd much like a sheriff that didn't think that way. I just don't like being on his list of potential bad guys."

The problem was, Sue had a point. I'd had a public confrontation with Blake in Tiny's. I'd had a nasty argument with him out at the job site. And a few hours later the man turned up dead.

I *did* make a good suspect.

CHAPTER 21

I left Sue's shop in a funk. What she said made a lot of sense, unfortunately. If the sheriff thought I was a suspect, I had bigger problems than Stan Fischer's job offer.

Walking back up Main Street to retrieve the Beetle, I considered the options. Certainly I could talk to the sheriff, maybe even convince him I wasn't the one that killed Blake Weston. I didn't consider that a likely scenario.

Sure, he hadn't picked me up, or had me brought in for more questions or anything. But that didn't mean he wouldn't. And if what I'd told him so far wasn't changing his mind, how could I expect anything else would?

Not unless I could give him a good reason to believe me. Like the name of the person who had really done it.

I was suspicious of Gregory, although I didn't want to accuse anyone. And Sue was right about one thing. I didn't like the man, and I would be glad of most anything that came between him and my mother.

Gregory was too much like Blake. And look how that one had turned out for me.

I started the Bug and pulled away from the curb. Curiosity made me turn at the next corner and cruise past the sheriff's office. Stan's Lincoln was parked in the front lot. It made sense that the sheriff would need more time with Stan, since he was the one who knew what Blake was doing in Pine Ridge.

Besides, Stan had told me he talked to Blake the night before he died. Stan might have been the last person to talk to him.

Except the murderer, of course.

I shook off the thought and turned the corner toward home. The dogs would be expecting a walk, and I wanted to get out and stretch my legs.

A walk would be good.

Thinking on my feet was usually a good way to work out whatever problems were running through my head. Not this time. I walked and thought and muttered.

I tried to figure out who would have something to gain from Blake Weston's death, but I had been away too long. I no longer knew the same people Blake did. I didn't know what he did or where he went.

I was the only one in Pine Ridge who knew Blake Weston, and I didn't know him at all.

And I was the one who needed to find his killer. It might be the sheriff's job, but I was the one with the most to lose.

Now all I needed was a plan.

That was a problem. Worse, my suspect list had only one name on it: Gregory Whitlock.

I would have to start with what I had, which wasn't much. Gregory had asked a lot of questions about Blake. It was time he started answering some of mine.

I didn't expect Gregory to answer anything directly, of course. I would have to get around him somehow, find the information I wanted without letting him know I suspected him.

There was only one place where I could easily get information about Gregory Whitlock. I had to go to my mother's house, and I couldn't let her know what I was up to.

It wouldn't be easy. I seldom went to Mom's house, and usually only when I was badgered into it.

Once the dogs were settled, I put my plan into action.

Getting to Mom's house was the easy

part. But if I wanted to get the real dirt on Gregory, I would have to be able to search the house without her knowing, which meant being there while she was gone.

That part wasn't so easy.

I had no idea what kind of information there might be at Mom's house, but I hoped there would be papers or records of some kind. After all, they were in business together, and they were, well, doing some other things together.

That was another problem. I might find things I didn't want to know about. In fact, the thought was so creepy I almost chickened out. But if I didn't find out who killed Blake, I was in danger of being the top candidate.

Besides, even if Gregory wasn't the culprit, he was asking a lot of questions. He had to know *something,* and I had to start my search somewhere.

I still had a key to my mother's house, and there were boxes of my things in the attic. But I didn't want to risk running into her — or Gregory. I would have to call her first, and make sure neither one of them was there.

I dialed Mom's cell phone and held my breath.

"Georgiana! Hello, dear." I could hear

traffic noise in the background, and the throaty purr of the Escalade at cruising speed. "What can I do for you?"

It galled me that she acted as though the only time I called her was when I needed something. What stung more, though, was that she was right. We didn't have the kind of relationship where we called each other just to chat, or palled around together.

We never went to the latest chick flick together, or lunched just for the fun of it, and we never, *ever* went shopping together. She was strictly Pearl District and I was outlet mall. The two did not mix well.

"Hi, Mom. Where are you?"

She sighed, audible through the hands-free connection. "Back to the Commons, I'm afraid. We had to have the landscapers come back, even though it's Saturday and they charge a ridiculous amount of money for weekends. There's still an issue, and I have to stand over them as if they're a bunch of five-year-olds to get the job done right."

She muttered something very unladylike at a passing motorist, then turned her attention back to me. "So, what can I do for you, dear?"

"This is going to sound crazy, but do you still have that box of kitchen stuff you gave me when I first moved back to Pine Ridge? I know I left it at your house while I was getting settled, and I don't think I ever picked it up."

"Hello? Who is this? You're using my daughter's cell phone, but it can't be my daughter. She said she had no use for 'all that kitchen junk' when I offered it to her."

I forced myself to laugh at her jibe. "No, Mother, it really is me. It's hard to believe, I know, but you can blame Wade. He made dinner at my house last night, and he made it clear my kitchen was not properly equipped."

"Is that all it takes?" I could picture her lifting one eyebrow and pursing her perfectly lipsticked mouth. "Remind me to enlist Wade's assistance the next time I try to help you."

"It's not like that, Mom." I was not going to have this argument. I just wanted her to say I could go get the box from the house, so I would have an excuse to look around.

"We'll have to talk about this later, dear. I'm here and I need to go straighten out the landscapers before the situation gets any worse."

"Mom, wait. If the box is at the house — if you still have it — I can just swing by and pick it up." I played my trump card. "I'm trying to do better in the kitchen, and I thought maybe the stuff you had would help."

Her tone softened. "You do need to eat better, dear. The box is in the attic. Go ahead and help yourself."

She hung up, but not before I heard her rattle off a lightning-fast string of Spanish orders. I felt sorry for the landscapers, but I told myself it was better them than me.

Phase One of Operation Gregory was complete.

I promised the dogs I'd be back soon, and headed out. It was early afternoon, prime time for real estate agents. I suspected that had something to do with Mom's annoyance at having to babysit the landscape crew at the Commons. It meant someone else would be in the office fielding calls and making the all-important first customer contact.

Someone like Gregory Whitlock.

At least that was what I hoped, because it would mean Gregory wasn't at my mother's house.

The driveway was empty and the garage door was closed when I got there. I parked in front, rang the doorbell and listened to the chimes echo through the empty house before I used my key and let myself in the front door.

The house was silent. I walked through into the kitchen and checked the garage door. Locked. I opened it and glanced at the empty garage, reassuring myself that I was alone. I relocked the door. If anyone came home while I was searching it might give me a few extra seconds to cover my tracks.

I tried not to think too much about what I was planning to do. This was my mother, and here I was sneaking into her house — yeah, I had a key, but since I was there under false pretenses I didn't think it really counted — and getting ready to go through her personal belongings.

There was a stalker quality to my actions that I didn't want to examine too closely.

I knew Mom had a home office, which is where I expected to find what I wanted, but it was in the back of the house, where I would have the most warning if someone came home.

I started with the kitchen. I'd seen a lot of that room over the last few months. Mom was determined that Gregory and I become friends, and she had made a regular practice of inviting me for dinner with them. She also made a practice of including Wade, fostering her not-so-secret agenda of encouraging our relationship.

I didn't need to check most of the cupboards and drawers, since I ended up helping in the kitchen each time we had dinner. My mother expected the women to do the cooking while the men relaxed. It was one of the reasons she despaired of my kitchen. For once, that had worked to my advantage.

Mom still had a tiny household office in an alcove of the kitchen. One beat-up two-drawer filing cabinet — a hand-me-down from my dad's first office — a simple counter, and a wicker chair painted a blazing white.

Standing in front of the file cabinet, I was directly in the line of sight of anyone who opened the garage door. If someone came in, I would only have a few seconds to put everything away.

I started with the bottom drawer. Several years of routine household expenses, utility bills, receipts for repairs and upkeep. Each year was in a separate section with its own individually labeled folders. The second drawer was more of the same, and everything was several years old. It was as though she had abandoned the office when she had been forced to abandon her ideal job of being the perfect wife.

No help.

The sideboard in the dining room held only china, silver, and linens, not that I expected anything else. Ditto the bookshelves and entertainment center in the living room.

I went down the hall toward the back of the house. I didn't bother with the guest bathroom in the hallway, but I did stop long enough to pull down the folding staircase that led to the attic. I wanted to be able to retreat up those stairs as quickly as possible if I needed to.

I glanced in the old guest bedroom. We'd never had very many actual guests, but that's what we always called it. The house didn't have a den or family room, so the guest room had been my de facto playroom when I was small, and my TV retreat as a teenager.

Now my mother had transformed it into a tiny home gym, complete with a top-of-the-line elliptical machine, a rack of hand weights, mirrors, and a flat-screen TV. She had removed the closet doors and filled the space with polished chrome racks piled with fluffy white towels, and a gleaming stainless-steel clothes hamper.

There wasn't anywhere to hide anything in that room.

I moved on.

My old bedroom was across the hall, the door slightly ajar. I pushed the door and stepped into Mom's new office. There was a massive rolltop desk I recognized as having been my father's. The satin-finished cherrywood glowed warmly, the way it had in Dad's office when I was a kid. A sleek notebook computer rested alone on the desktop. Of course Mom would have everything neatly filed away.

Many of our older clients at Samurai had been fearful of new technology. Despite the obvious advantages, they had to be coaxed into the world of high tech.

My mother was the exact opposite. From what I had seen, she had enthusiastically embraced the twenty-first century, and turned each new piece of technology to her advantage. Her laptop, PDA, cell phone, and GPS were all part of the technological arsenal that kept her in the top rank at Whitlock Estates.

It also meant there might be useful information on her laptop. I should be able to hack into her files without much trouble, but there might be an easier way. Maybe I should just offer to give her the benefit of that expensive education she was always talking about.

This might be my only chance at the office, however.

I glanced at my watch. I'd already been in the house fifteen minutes, and I hadn't found anything. If any of the neighbors noticed, Mom might wonder what had taken me so long.

I opened doors and pulled out drawers in a hasty search. There were boxes of discs, each neatly labeled in a code that wasn't immediately apparent.

My frustration grew. Mom had all her files backed up on disc, but there was no way I could go through them in the time I had.

The credenza was another matter. I found a file with loan papers for the house, showing a second mortgage taken out three years ago, right after she got her real estate license. Along with the loan documents was a list of payments made from the escrow, including a payment to Whitlock Estates referenced to "Clackamas Commons."

Had she loaned Gregory money? Was she repaying a loan from his company? Did he hold an interest in her house somehow, or she an interest in his?

I looked at the closed door at the end of the hallway — my mother's bedroom. I shook my head. I wasn't that desperate.

Yet.

I heard a car in the driveway, and the

groan of the garage door opening.

I shoved the file folder back in place, slammed the drawer shut, and raced into the hall and up the staircase to the attic.

I dug frantically through the piles of sealed cartons, each labeled in my mother's precise handwriting with the contents and the date.

It struck me that mom's organizational skills and rigid control were wasted as a housewife. She could have planned the D-day invasion and pulled it off without a hitch.

I spotted the box I needed. It said "Georgiana — Kitchen Equipment" with a date just a week after I had moved into the rental in Pine Ridge. Apparently the box had gone in the attic, labeled and dated, just days after I'd told her I wasn't ready for it yet.

My shirt sleeve caught a cobweb as I hefted the box into my arms. I left it there as evidence of my search in the attic.

Cradling the box in my arms, I took a few steps down the staircase and waited. The door from the garage to the kitchen opened, and I called out, "Mom, is that you?"

"No, Georgiana, it's me," a male voice called back.

Gregory. I nearly lost my grip on the box. The contents rattled as the box shifted, a tinny clattering sound.

Gregory appeared in the hallway. His expression was bland, but there was a hint of self-satisfaction in his eyes, as though "catching" me in the house was an accomplishment.

"Here," he said, "let me take that for you."

I handed over the box, feeling exposed without it in my arms. How had Gregory managed to show up at the house, just at the time I was there? On a day he should be working? Was he spying on me somehow?

CHAPTER 22

Gregory carried the box into the kitchen and set it down on the empty counter. My mother's kitchen was always so spotless, you could eat off the floor — though I never understood why anyone would want to.

I made a show of opening the box and rummaging through the contents, while Gregory watched. "Mom said there were some things in here I needed," I chattered, trying to disguise the nervousness that made my knees feel shaky.

If I was right, Gregory had something to do with the death of Blake Weston. I was alone with a man I suspected of involvement with a murder. No wonder I felt nervous.

I pulled out a soup ladle. "This is what I was looking for," I said. I held it for a moment, wondering if I could use it as a weapon to defend myself.

Not really. I dropped it back in the box

with the other kitchen gear, and folded the top down. I could always throw the entire box at him and run. Sue said that running was a good solution, and this instant I couldn't think of a better one.

Unfortunately, Gregory was between me and the doorway.

He moved forward a step. "Really too bad about your friend," he said. "I hear the sheriff's calling it a murder, not an accident."

He took another step. "Did you ever find out what he was here for?"

I stood my ground. Mostly because there wasn't anywhere to go. I breathed deep and balanced myself on the balls of my feet, ready to move.

"A job, as far as I know, Gregory. Like I told you and Mom the other day, he was designing a security system for the Mc-Comb project. We only exchanged a few words."

"A pretty heated few words, from what I was told. I hear you called him some names and he made some nasty remarks."

He shrugged and took another step. "That sounds like a lot more than just someone you used to work with.

"It sounds like you two had a much more personal relationship."

He was almost close enough to reach out and touch me. The box was on the counter next to me. I could run and leave it there, though I wasn't sure how I'd explain that to my mother.

That was the least of my worries.

"It was a small company. We worked under extreme pressure and for long hours. Everything felt personal after a while." Not a great excuse, but I had other things on my mind.

Like my mother's murderous boyfriend.

Gregory shrugged elaborately this time, lifting his hands and raising his shoulders. "I suppose." He smiled, an expression that sent another chill through me. "I know we get that same feeling at Whitlock Estates. Although" — his tone shifted to embarrassed amusement — "some of the relationships actually become personal."

His glance toward the doorway leading to the dining room and the bedrooms beyond underscored exactly how personal one of those relationships had become. The parallel with my relationship with Blake wasn't lost on me.

Did Gregory know anything about me and Blake? Or was he fishing for information?

Was he worried that Blake might have given me information that would implicate

238

him as his killer?

"Ancient history," I said with a lightness I didn't feel. "I don't know exactly what you heard, but we had a few words and that was it. I went back to work, and he went away. Last I saw of him."

I didn't count the image I couldn't get out of my head: flashlights illuminating a pair of hand-stitched Italian loafers in the mud at the bottom of the moat.

Gregory reached toward me. I put my arms up in a defensive pose, ready to repel his attack.

He gave me a quizzical look as he hefted the box of kitchen gear into his arms. "Let me carry this out to your car for you."

I pretended I was reaching for the box, then dropped my arms and said "Thanks," hoping I had covered my initial reaction. Gregory shrugged and turned away.

I followed him through the dining room and into the living room. I glanced at the hall where the attic staircase still extended down from the ceiling.

"I'll take care of the ladder," he said.

I didn't argue. All I wanted was to get out of the house and away from Gregory as fast as I could.

The evening stretched in front of me. I

could call Sue, but I hesitated. What if she had plans with the sheriff? It was Saturday night, date night.

The kitchen was full of food, the refrigerator was stocked, and I had a box full of new-to-me kitchen tools. I wasn't being a recluse; I was reacquainting myself with my kitchen.

I unpacked and scrubbed the tools, and put them away. Underneath the spatulas and ladles and spoons I found baking pans — two round cake pans, a ceramic pie plate with a cover, a pair of loaf pans. I wondered if I even remembered how to bake bread — a skill my mother had insisted was necessary for any good homemaker to master.

Not that I was going to try it tonight. But who knew what the new, more domestic Georgie might do?

Daisy and Buddha were confused by my sudden burst of domesticity. They followed me around the house, whining at the vacuum and whimpering when the bathroom cleaner stung their noses. They approved of the kitchen duties, though. It meant the three of us hung out in the room with food, and they might occasionally get a scrap or two.

Cooking didn't distract me enough. I wanted to know why Blake Weston, a man who never even ventured into the suburbs, had traveled to a place he would have considered the edge of civilization. Even a job as big as the McComb project wouldn't have been enough to tempt him.

There had to be more to it. I knew where to look, I just didn't want to.

I got my laptop, set it on the kitchen table, and booted up. Within minutes I was on the Samurai Security website, looking at their latest achievements.

I had resisted the temptation to even look at their site since I left San Francisco. There was something slightly ghoulish about looking at the site of a company I used to own.

I had put it all behind me, and refused to turn back. But Blake's death was forcing me to revisit the past.

There were no links from the website to the Samurai computers. It would have been beyond embarrassing for anyone to gain access to the internal system. The site's servers were run from an independent web-hosting company. No way to reach the Samurai company records directly.

The phone rang and I heard Stan Fischer's booming voice. "Georgie Girl, it's Stan. Just got through with the McCombs. Took a little longer than I expected. I'm headed back to my hotel." He cleared his throat and waited for me to pick up.

I did.

"Hi, Stan."

"Sorry about dinner, but your friend the sheriff kept me longer than I expected. He had an awful lot of questions about you and Blake. Sounds like the two of you got into some kind of shouting match. I think I settled him down, though. Told him you and Blake were old news, that I was sure what he'd heard was exaggerated. Then I had to go make nice with the McCombs."

"They're good people, Stan, that shouldn't be too hard."

"Wouldn't be," he agreed, "if they weren't anxious about getting the preliminary work on the security system. Blake was supposed to have something for them by the time he flew home, which would have been Tuesday.

"Now it looks like that will get delayed, but they aren't willing to wait long."

"You guys are the best, Stan. Chad knows that, or he wouldn't have hired you."

"That may be," he said. "But I was hoping you would reconsider my offer."

"I'm not current on the technology, Stan."

"Just do a walk-through with me," he wheedled. "The sheriff says we can go out there Monday. I'll pay you consultant rates for the couple hours it'll take, and you can write up a preliminary report. That's all I

242

need, the initial assessment. I know," he added, before I could protest, "I could get one of the guys up here. But you can do this standing on your head, and it will save me pulling somebody off another project and dumping them into this one cold."

I replayed the conversation in my head. Stan was better at political maneuvering than I had given him credit for. He had been reasonably subtle, but the message was clear: I vouched for you with the sheriff, you bail me out on this project.

The McComb deal must be important to Samurai for Stan to put the pressure on an employee they had dumped. And I needed to find out why before I went out to the site on Monday.

"Well, if it's really only a couple hours, Stan. I have another job, you know. Wouldn't want my boss to think I was slacking off on it."

"Not a chance with you, Georgie Girl. I know how hard you work, and I'm sure he does, too."

We made plans to meet with Chad Mc-Comb at the job site at 7:00 A.M. Monday morning. Stan said he was hoping to get done and catch an afternoon flight back to San Francisco. He'd already been away longer than he had planned.

I rushed to end the conversation and get back to my research. With the walk-through scheduled for early Monday morning, I had a lot to do in the next twenty-four hours.

An hour later, the Internet had yielded little actual information on Samurai Security. There were occasional press releases about one project or another, and an industry award for solving a denial-of-service attack on a financial firm.

But nothing about the company itself. The business dealings of Samurai Security were as unreachable as the company's files.

There was another option. I remembered Richard Parks's phone calls. I hadn't ratted on him, but I did have some leverage. And I didn't think I could use it effectively over the phone.

This required a face-to-face meeting.

What had the sheriff said about traveling? Not to plan any long trips? That certainly wasn't the case. In fact, if I played this right, I would be back before anyone knew I was gone.

I jumped from the news-archive site to a discount-travel site, searching for last-minute airfares. I found a single seat on a crack-of-dawn hop the next morning to San Francisco, returning the same evening.

I looked at my bank balance, and cringed.

Enough to pay the utilities and eat the rest of the month, with nothing left over for a sudden trip to San Francisco.

I pulled out my credit card. It was only for emergencies, and I had managed to avoid using it. But if the threat of being arrested for murder wasn't an emergency, then I couldn't think of anything that was. Besides, with a little luck the Samurai consulting fee should cover the costs.

If and when I got the check.

When I left for the airport in the morning it was still dark. When I hit I-205 it was almost deserted, and I made it to the airport in near-record time.

I made a last check of my pockets for anything that would upset security, like a forgotten wrench or screwdriver, and hoisted my laptop bag over my shoulder. I had no plans that required the computer, but I felt naked going to San Francisco without it. It was my security blanket, my protective prop that said I belonged.

The long corridor from the parking garage to the terminal was empty, a cold, echoing tunnel that had me looking over my shoulder every few steps.

No one knew my plans. I wasn't breaking any law. The sheriff hadn't told me not to leave town, he'd only suggested I not plan any long trips. San Francisco was only a couple hours' flight, and I would be back tonight. Still, I couldn't shake the feeling that someone was following me, watching where I went and what I did.

The terminal was nearly as deserted as the tunnel. I bypassed the luggage check in. I was only going for the day, and I had everything in my laptop case that was slung over my shoulder.

I took my boarding pass from my jacket pocket and presented it at the security gate. An unsmiling agent examined my pass and driver's license.

I tried to think of something to say to cheer him up, but ended up saying nothing. No telling what might trigger the suspicions of someone looking for shoe bombs.

It was never too early for Starbucks, and I joined the line at the counter just past the security checkpoint. A few minutes later I had a mocha with an extra shot and a pastry. The perfect breakfast: sugar, chocolate, and caffeine.

The plane was only about half full; no one with any choice in the matter was going to take a 6:00 A.M. flight on a Sunday morning. But it meant I got a row to myself, and I was able to leave the laptop in its case instead of opening it and using it as a shield against a seatmate who wanted to chatter for the entire two hours.

I leafed through a magazine, trying to distract myself from the task ahead. I had to find Richard Parks, which should be fairly easy since he'd left his cell number with me.

Then I had to persuade him to talk to me. Also not too difficult. But getting him to tell me what I wanted might be a little trickier. He was already concerned that he had said too much, and now I would want more.

I had that to use as leverage, and I had one other thing: I was sure that when I was dating Blake, Richard had a crush on me. It meant he might be more willing to talk, but I wouldn't use it to trick him. Not the way Blake had used my feelings for him to trick me. If I did that I was no better than the man I had come to despise.

It was ironic. I was spending money I couldn't afford — money I hoped I might be able to recoup from Samurai — to chase information on the murder of a man I hated. I was giving up my time and putting myself in jeopardy to find his killer.

Even after his death, Blake Weston was messing up my life.

CHAPTER 23

In the San Francisco International terminal I caught the BART into the city. An hour after landing I was standing at the Powell Street station. The Bush Avenue address Blake had used was only a few blocks away.

I pulled out my cell phone and called the number Richard had left for me. I hoped Richard wasn't the type to sleep late on Sunday morning. From what I remembered of him, it didn't seem likely.

He answered on the third ring, his voice froggy but alert.

"Georgiana? Is that you?"

"Yes, Richard, it's me. I, uh, I wondered if you could spare a few minutes to talk to me. I know it's short notice, but I'd really like to get some information from you." I paused, giving him time to answer. When he didn't I continued. "I could have asked Stan yesterday, of course. But it might have been awkward to try to explain how I knew about things down here."

"No good deed, and all that, huh?"

"It's not like that, Richard. I think there were some rumors spread around, and I'd like the chance to set the record straight. And maybe find out how they got started in the first place.

"It won't take long, honest."

He sighed. "Can it wait until I've had my coffee?"

"Sure. But I have a better idea." I couldn't help pausing a moment, playing the drama queen. "How about we meet for breakfast?"

"What?!"

"I'm standing outside the Powell Street station, just a few blocks from the address Blake was using. I flew in this morning."

"Well, if you flew down here just to talk to me . . ."

"I did, Richard. I thought this might be something that would be better in person than over the phone."

"OK. Let me check with my wife." He was gone before I could voice my surprise at that news. Guess I wasn't playing the crush card.

Richard was back on the phone in a minute or so. "Barb says she would love to meet the famous Georgiana Neverall, if it's okay for her to come along."

I didn't answer immediately, and Richard sensed my hesitation. "There are no secrets between us, Georgie. None." His emphasis told me I was famous for more than my hasty departure from Samurai.

"Then sure, as long as you're willing to talk to me with her there."

Richard said he was, and suggested a small restaurant near Union Square. It had been a popular spot for breakfast with the Samurai crew when we'd pulled all-nighters.

"You still in the neighborhood then?" I asked.

"A tiny, overpriced condo," he answered. "But it's walking distance to the office. Without a car, it's almost affordable," he finished with a laugh.

We agreed to meet in an hour, and I flipped my phone closed. I had a little time to kill in a city I hadn't seen in several years. It was more time than I needed to saunter the few blocks to Union Square, and not nearly enough to get reacquainted with the city I had loved.

I walked toward Union Square. The sun was up, and the fog was beginning to burn off. The day promised to be clear, but cool.

I'd dressed for the weather in tan cords, low-heeled boots, and a wool jacket — the practical remnants of my San Francisco wardrobe. One good thing about the work I'd done all summer, it kept me in shape. I could still wear the few good pieces I'd kept when I left the city, and simple pants and classically tailored jackets never went out of style.

I wandered through the streets of upscale shopping, glancing in windows and occasionally stopping to admire a pair of shoes or a piece of jewelry in a window. The displays were dazzling, an elegant collection of winter colors and styles hinting at the cold weather to come.

A camel-colored wool coat caught my eye and I stopped. The cut was perfect, and the fabric looked soft. I could imagine the brush of the collar against my cheek.

Then I thought about cleaning bills, and a camel-colored coat covered with dog hair, and the smell of wet wool when the Great North-wet went into the rainy season.

Gore-Tex was more my style now.

I passed in front of a shop specializing in glass and crystal where I'd bought Blake a pair of champagne flutes to celebrate some milestone we had shared.

Not all the memories were bad. Still, those two glasses probably cost more than all the dishes and glassware in my current kitchen.

Many of the shops weren't open yet, but

it didn't matter. I wasn't there to buy, though I could still admire the beauty of the clothes and accessories displayed.

I still liked beautiful things — like the crystal wine glasses in the window. Perhaps when I solved my current financial dilemma I could buy an occasional bauble just to treat myself.

I checked my watch — the good gold one this time — and headed toward the twenty-four-hour diner on Sutter. Richard and his wife should be there soon, but I wanted to be there before them.

Somehow it felt like it would give me some control over our conversation, and I could use all the help I could get. After all, with his wife along, they outnumbered me.

I took a booth along the front window, where I would be able to see Richard as he approached. If he was on time I should only have a few minutes to wait.

The diner was as I remembered: all stainless steel, red-and-black vinyl, and gleaming-white tile. The booths were similar to the ones in Dee's, except these were replicas and Dee's were the real thing.

I couldn't remember if Stan had ever joined us in any of the predawn gatherings. Usually it was a small group of code monkeys and hardware wonks, punchy with exhaustion, crammed into a booth in the back of the diner. After the first time they knew to hide us from the normal customers. As if anyone who stumbled into a diner at 4:00 A.M. was very normal.

I didn't think Stan had ever been to the diner with us. He wasn't the type to fraternize with the kind of people he saw as eggheads. He did just fine with the guys driving trucks and pulling wire, or the other deep pockets on the board. But the people in between baffled him.

It was kind of amazing, actually, that he had taken a liking to me. But he was an early investor, and he knew my small-town background. Even with an advanced degree, I was still one of the real people.

I watched the people passing on the street as I waited. My palms were sweating, and my stomach knotted with each sip of coffee. I had deliberately walked into one of the places where I might run into someone I knew. It wasn't a happy thought.

I spotted Richard across the street, waiting for the light to change before he crossed. Relief flooded me. He had come, and he didn't have a crowd of Samurai employees — or police — with him.

If I hadn't been expecting him, he could have walked past without me recognizing

253

him. His standard uniform of discount center khaki pants, short-sleeved shirt, and white socks was gone. He wore designer jeans and a fisherman-knit sweater, with sneakers that didn't come from a discount store. His glasses were gone, though from a distance I couldn't tell if he was wearing contacts, or if he'd had surgery.

He was tall, well over six feet. But the last time I'd seen him he still looked like a puppy — all big feet and long legs that he hadn't yet grown into — his posture loose and sloppy. In the intervening years he had filled out and learned to stand up straight, though I suspected his companion might have something to do with the air of confidence he projected.

That was the biggest change — he wasn't alone. Standing next to him, her fingers entwined with his, was a striking woman. Nearly as tall as Richard, she had wavy red hair and the fair complexion to go with it. Even in jeans and a bulky sweater matching Richard's she turned heads on the sidewalk. For a split second I thought I might know her, but I dismissed the idea. Exhaustion and paranoia were making me see things that weren't there.

I suddenly felt both underdressed and overdressed at the same time. I hastily ran my fingers through my short hair, glancing at my reflection in the tinted front window. Too late to do anything about it now.

The couple crossed the street, the woman's stride matching Richard's. They were an imposing sight, and he didn't look at all like the tentative voice I'd heard on the phone.

Which one was the real Richard? And had I come all this way based on a voice, only to find someone who wasn't going to tell me what I needed to know?

They breezed through the door, the woman laughing up at Richard over some private joke they shared. He turned and caught sight of me, and rushed over, pulling her along.

"Georgie! It's so good to see you!"

For one awkward moment I thought he was going to try and hug me, even though I was still seated. The moment passed as he seemed to remember why we were there.

"Georgie, this is my wife, Barbara. Barb, this is Georgiana Neverall, the founder of Samurai."

Barbara extended her hand and I shook it briefly before she slid gracefully into the seat across from me. Richard slid in next to her, draping his arm over the back of the booth, his hand resting lightly on his wife's shoulder.

"Richard has told me so much about you," Barbara said. "I feel like I know you already."

I smiled in what I hoped was a friendly manner. "I didn't even know Richard was married. I've been a bit out of touch the last few years."

We chatted for a few minutes. I heard how they met and married. Richard told me proudly that Barbara was a lawyer.

I nearly spewed coffee across the table. "You brought your *lawyer?* I thought this was a friendly conversation."

"It is," he assured me. "She works for the City Attorney's office. Code enforcement, that kind of thing."

Barbara reached in her shoulder bag and produced a business card, identifying her as an investigator for the City Attorney's office.

We kept to relatively safe subjects until after our food arrived, and the waiter had drifted away. I kept glancing around, worried that we might be overheard.

"I suppose you want to know why I called you," I said.

"No," Richard replied. "Calling I understand. What I want to know is why you flew all the way down here. What was so important that you couldn't have talked to me on the phone?"

"Fair question. The truth is, I needed to get some answers fast — like yesterday. I was afraid you might not want to talk to me. I took a chance that you wouldn't say no if I flew down here to talk to you in person."

"Good guess," Barbara said.

"I hadn't counted on you," I said to her. "I just hoped I could get the information I needed and get back home tonight. Before anyone noticed I was gone."

"And you knew Richard was a sucker for you. Right, honey?" She elbowed her husband in the ribs and gave him a fond smile. "He had a huge crush on you, back in the day. Lucky for me, he still has a thing for older women."

Richard colored, reminding me of the awkward boy I had known still living deep inside. "You're not that much older than me, Barb," he protested.

"I'm beginning to think he's the lucky one," I said.

"Okay, you got me, Counselor," I continued. "I did think Richard would talk to me. But to be fair, he called me first."

"She's right, Barb. I started this." He turned to look at me. "So . . . back to my original question. What was so important that you flew down here instead of using the phone?"

"It's about this job. The McComb project. Stan asked me to do a walk-through with him tomorrow, but I'm not up on the current tech. I'm no longer qualified to do it, and I told him so. I couldn't mention your name, since I promised I wouldn't let him know I talked to you, but you should be doing this job.

"You need to call him and offer to fly up. Tell him you know Blake's work — which you do, or at least you did — and you can rearrange your schedule to come up immediately."

"I can't."

"What do you mean you can't? Of course you can. Heck, you could have had my job in a nanosecond if you wanted it."

I shoved aside my plate, and poured another cup of coffee from the carafe on the table. Before I went on. "I'm not saying I wasn't good. I was. But you could work rings around me, you were that much better."

I stopped and cocked my head to one side, looking at him.

"By the way, *do* you have my job?"

"No. Nobody does. When you left there

was a reshuffle of duties and parts of the job went to three or four different people. Whole place is different now."

Richard shifted uncomfortably in his seat, and frowned. The conversation clearly bothered him.

"So why can't you do this, Richard? You're the best person for the job. I'm not. Not anymore. Stan said he'd pay me as a consultant, but you'd be better."

"I wouldn't, Georgie. Believe me." Richard glanced sideways at his wife. She arched her eyebrows at him and nodded. "You might as well tell her," she said. "You know you're going to."

He looked back at me. "I'm not supposed to know this, but I have some friends in the controller's office. There's a cash crunch. Nothing critical, they say. Don't worry about it.

"But I know Blake was concerned, and Stan was in Blake's office a lot the last couple weeks. Rumor was they were courting some big investor. Millionaire, I heard.

"I think part of Blake's job on this trip was to seal the deal for the cash we need. And that's the part I can't do."

I let the information sift into my brain. A few more pieces of the puzzle fell into place. It explained Blake's buddy act with Chad and Astrid at Tiny's, and Stan flying in to take over instead of sending one of the tech crew.

The contact with McComb was more than a job. And more than a possible expansion to the Northwest.

Samurai was fishing for money, looking for an investor with deep pockets. The same deep pockets I suspected Gregory Whitlock wanted to pick.

"You didn't talk to Blake at all while he was up there, did you? I seem to recall you said you hadn't spoken to him directly."

"I did talk to him once. That was when he told me he'd seen you, but he hadn't had a chance to actually talk to you."

I thought for a minute. "This might sound kind of strange," I said, "but did he say anything about asking me to come back to Samurai?"

Richard chewed on his bottom lip for a moment, his brow furrowed as he tried to recall his conversation with Blake. He shook his head. "No, not exactly. He did say we should have tried to talk you out of resigning, and we should do something about it — that we needed you.

"But he'd said things like that all along."

His mouth twisted and a note of apology crept into his tone. "He was angry when you left, Georgie. Said you made your choice, or something like that.

"He said you didn't really care about Samurai. All you wanted was the money."

CHAPTER 24

"What money? This supposed buyout?"

Heads turned from nearby tables, and I realized I had shouted. My face grew hot, and I clutched my coffee cup in my fist. I forced myself to speak more softly. "There wasn't any money! Blake started those rumors as a cover-up."

Richard hesitated. He looked around, making sure our neighbors had gone back to their own business before he answered.

"I don't think Blake started those rumors, Georgie. He was angry, yes. But it wasn't a show. You could tell when Blake was faking. He didn't think we could, but the people that were around him knew."

"I couldn't," I muttered. I could taste the bitterness in my words. "He had me completely fooled."

"Maybe not," Richard said softly. "I think he really was upset when you left. He said he felt betrayed and he got upset whenever someone mentioned you."

I shook my head. "There's just one small problem with that, Richard. *He* dumped *me*. On voice mail. Wouldn't even talk to me — just left a message and refused to answer the phone when I called him."

Richard shrugged. It was clear he didn't agree with me. I wasn't going to convince him. He wasn't going to convince me. There was no use discussing it.

I decided to try another tack.

"If Blake didn't start those rumors, then who did? Who had anything to gain by making me look bad?"

"Nobody. But the way I heard it . . ." he glanced at his wife and she nodded her encouragement.

"She has a right to know, Rick."

His head bobbed in agreement, and looked back at me. "I heard the news was leaked by the board. They didn't want to talk about your resignation, not officially. But the word got around. You took a big pile of cash and walked away."

"And you all believed it?" I clenched my hands into fists, my fingernails digging into my palms. I concentrated on breathing, focused on the task at hand. I pushed away the anger that washed over me when I thought everyone believed I would abandon the company I started.

Richard squirmed. "Not so much, at first. But then nobody heard from you, and it got easier to believe until I finally stopped *not* believing."

He shook his head, his voice pleading. "For a long time I wanted to think there was another reason."

Barbara reached for his hand and squeezed it. She looked across at me, and I caught a glint of fierce protectiveness in her eyes. She dared me to argue with him.

"I don't blame you. At least you called me when you heard about Blake. I appreciate that. Really."

Barbara seemed to accept my statement, and I went on. "But there was never any buyout. Blake left me a voice mail late one night, and I got called in early the next morning and Stan offered me the chance to resign before the board fired me."

Somehow it didn't hurt as much to say it this time. Maybe I had just repeated it enough times that I was numb. Or maybe the whole mess had lost its ability to cause me pain. For whatever reason, having it out in the open was becoming easier each time I revealed the truth.

Richard looked stunned. "I never heard anything like that. And I don't think Blake knew anything about it. I mean, why would he say we shouldn't have let you resign and we should do something about it? He couldn't have known."

I shrugged. "It's what he would be expected to say."

"He meant it." Richard sat straight and looked me in the eye. His gaze held steady. "He didn't know."

"So you think the rumors came from the board?"

"I know they did."

We sat for a minute without speaking. Several tables near us were now filled by chattering groups enjoying a Sunday breakfast out. The buzz of conversation washed over our quiet table, carried along with the rich fragrance of continually brewing pots of coffee.

There was one more topic I had to broach. I tried to find a graceful way to slide it into the conversation, but nothing came to mind.

I nearly jumped out of my skin when my cell phone rang. I hastily fished it out of my bag and glanced at the display.

Wade.

I frowned. "Sorry, I have to take this."

I tried to keep the conversation short. Wade suggested we have brunch at a restaurant a few miles north of Pine Ridge. I of course turned him down, but he persisted.

Finally, I admitted I wasn't in town. "There was someone I needed to see," I said. "I'll be back later this afternoon."

I did some mental arithmetic. "How about we meet for dinner?"

"Georgie." There was an uneasy pause. "Where are you?"

"I don't think you want to know."

"Yes, I do."

"No. Really. You don't. Trust me on this."

The silence at the other end of the line stretched long enough that I thought I'd lost the call. I held the phone away from my ear and checked. The call timer continued clicking off the seconds of silence. That was a bad sign.

Wade sighed. "When will you be back?"

"Late this afternoon. So dinner would be fine," I said brightly.

Wade didn't believe it. "Georgie," he said slowly, "just where did you go?"

"To see an old friend. Someone who might be able to help me figure out what happened. Okay?"

"Not okay." He sighed again. "I'm not going to get an answer before dinner, am I?"

"Nope. I'll meet you at Tiny's at seven."

I hung up before he could say anything more.

I'd managed to stay calm while I was on the phone, but once the connection was broken my hands started to shake. I could barely manage to get the phone back in my bag. Both Richard and Barbara stared at me. In the end, Richard stretched one long arm across the table and held the bag steady, while I dropped the phone in its pocket.

"Your boyfriend?" Barbara asked.

I nodded. "Sort of. I think."

"You didn't tell him where you were going, did you?"

"It is that obvious?" I hung my head. "I'm afraid I'm not very good at this."

"At what?" Richard asked, his expression puzzled. "Boyfriends?"

I laughed harshly. After watching my experience with Blake, he should know the answer to that one.

"No."

This was the place where I would have told them to sit down, but they were already sitting. There was no way to ease into it. I blurted out, "The sheriff says Blake Weston was murdered."

Richard's mouth formed a silent O of surprise and his eyes grew wide.

Barbara seemed to take the news more calmly. "That's not what that call was about, though."

I shook my head. "I knew before I came down."

She waited a few seconds, then asked, "And?"

"And what?" Richard said. His voice was thin and reedy, and he looked pasty, as though he was in shock.

"And why did she fly all the way down here? To tell us that? You would have heard at work tomorrow, or she could have given you the news over the phone." She turned to me. "Right?"

I nodded. "Absolutely. But there are some things that don't add up. And there's another complication.

"I think the sheriff suspects me."

"Ridiculous!" Richard had regained his voice. "What possible reason could you have? You and Blake were history."

I winced. "That's what I thought. But Blake showed up at the site where I was working — I'm on the construction crew at the McComb site — and we had" — I hesitated — "words."

Barbara nodded. "A public argument, right? And he turned up dead just a few hours later? Yeah, that doesn't look good."

She gave me a hard look. "Does the *sheriff* know you're down here?"

"I didn't tell him, either," I said, remembering the feeling of being watched in the airport. I hoped he didn't know I'd left the area, but I couldn't be sure.

"He didn't tell me I couldn't leave town, he just said not to plan any long trips. I'll be back in a few hours." I heard a note of defensiveness in my voice, even though I wasn't doing anything wrong. Exactly.

Barbara chuckled. "You ever consider becoming a lawyer? You sure got that letter-of-the-law thing down."

I looked at Richard. For the first time, some of what had happened made sense. No one tried to reach me because they thought I'd left them and deserted the company. The board got rid of me, and blamed me at the same time.

No wonder Stan offered me the chance to resign. If this is what happened when I left "voluntarily," I didn't want to see what a real fight would look like.

The sidewalk outside the diner was crowded with shoppers, and every table inside was full. We had lingered far longer than was expected, and the waiter was checking more frequently.

Richard looked around, surveying the crowd. It was time for us to leave.

I tugged my credit card from my pocket

and reached for the check. Richard pulled it away before my hand closed around it.

"This one's on me, Georgie. Consider it an apology for believing the things I heard."

"You don't have to do that. I invited you." My protest sounded weak, and it was. I'd be paying for this trip for several months if the Samurai consulting fee didn't materialize.

He shook his head. "My treat. You get the check when I come visit you."

"Yeah. Like that'll happen."

"It could. Especially if we still do this Mc-Comb job." He grinned. "You're the one that wants me to come do the work so you don't have to."

He had a point. I did want him to come do the job, because there was no way I could.

We shook hands on the sidewalk, with promises to keep in touch. Maybe we even meant it.

I told Barbara how delighted I'd been to meet her. I did mean that. It was good to see that someone had come out of Samurai with a successful relationship. Blake and I certainly hadn't, and it sounded as though Stan Fischer had lost another marital round.

At least somebody was happy.

CHAPTER 25

I was early getting back to the airport, so of course my flight was delayed. I used the time to open up my laptop and do some research.

Once I knew what to look for, the signs were there. The Samurai press releases were relentlessly upbeat — like those of any other company — but now it felt like they were trying to hide bad news.

I checked up on Blake Weston, Stan Fischer, and the other directors whose names I could remember. Occasionally a society story would link a familiar name to Stan and I would have another lead to follow.

I had a long list of places to look by the time they called my flight. I waited until the rest of the flight was boarded, then shut my laptop, shoved it in the case, and claimed my seat.

I'd allowed for delays when I made my

plans to meet Wade, but I was still running late. I called him as soon as I ransomed the Beetle from the parking garage and headed east.

The connection was poor, but Wade's annoyance came through loud and clear. I hung up and prayed to the traffic gods.

I sped along I-205 and wheeled off at the Sunnyside exit. My hands gripped the wheel tightly, and I pushed the tiny four-banger to its limit. Wade and I had been a couple for a few months in high school. When I went away to college we lost touch. Now that I was back we were still trying to figure out if we were a thing or not, and lately I was hoping we were.

But I seemed to be a magnet for trouble, and Wade was a politician with prospects. The combination could prove difficult for both of us.

I zipped into the lot at Tiny's with about two minutes to spare. I finger-combed my hair, thankful that the short cut — practical for work — required minimum care for a dinner date.

My cords and jacket were a bit overdressed for Tiny's but I hoped Wade wouldn't notice. At least the dark boots would be right at home in the tavern.

I didn't see Wade's hybrid in the parking

lot, and I breathed a sigh of relief. If I got here first he couldn't really complain about me being late.

I said a quick thank-you to the gods of traffic and went inside.

Someone was waiting for me, but it wasn't Wade.

It was the sheriff. And he didn't look at all happy to see me. In fact, he looked downright peeved.

"Evening, Miss Neverall," he said stiffly. "Would you care to step outside with me?"

"I'm waiting for Councilman Montgomery," I answered with a charming smile. "We're having dinner."

The sheriff put a hand under my elbow. He had a grip like a pair of locking pliers. It would do me no good to try and pull away.

"Miss Neverall, I will ask you one more time. Would you care to step outside with me?"

The alternative, clearly, was going to be something unpleasant in front of everyone in Tiny's.

I turned and went back out the door, the sheriff clamped tightly on my arm.

Once we were outside, I protested his treatment. "What do you mean, grabbing me like that?" I kept my voice down so it didn't carry back inside. "What do you want that's so important you have to go around grabbing people?"

"Murder is what's so important, Neverall." I noticed he dropped the *Miss* now that we were out of earshot of the small crowd inside. "That, and people who run off when I tell them to stay around."

I opened my mouth, but he stopped me with a firm shake of his head. "Please do not say anything more."

Then, to my dismay, he began to recite my Miranda rights.

When he finished I stood there with my mouth open, unable to form a single coherent word.

"Do you understand these rights?" he repeated.

I nodded.

"Georgiana Neverall, I have a warrant to detain you as a material witness in the homicide of Blake Weston." He signaled to a car in the back of Tiny's lot, and an unmarked sedan cruised silently up to the driveway near where we stood.

"Come with me." He pulled me along toward the car and opened the back door. He stood so he blocked my path, should I get the idea I could run away.

I knew when I had no chance. I sat down in the backseat and watched him close the door on me.

Once he was seated in the front, he spoke without turning around. "Put on your seat belt, Neverall. Or I can come back there and do it for you."

I put on my seat belt.

The sheriff grunted his satisfaction with my cooperation and nodded to the deputy. We pulled out onto the deserted highway, leaving my Beetle with my laptop inside in the parking lot at Tiny's.

"Sheriff," I said softly, "my computer's in the car. Can we please check that it's locked before we go?"

"Turn around," he said to the deputy. He sounded as though forming the words was painful.

We pulled back in the lot, the deputy checked the locks on the Beetle and climbed back in behind the wheel.

"Locked." It was the only word he spoke the entire time.

The sheriff remained silent for the rest of the short drive and I decided it was probably my best option.

We arrived at the station to find a welcoming committee. Wade was there, his hair disheveled and his eyes dark with worry. My mother leaned on Gregory, as though she didn't have the strength to hold herself up.

Gregory played the part of the strong, supportive alpha-male boyfriend. He kept one arm around my mother's waist, a gesture of ownership more than protection.

Sue stood next to Wade. Her warring emotions played across her face, and I felt a pang of regret for the position I'd put her in. Her boyfriend had arrested her best friend, and no matter what she did she put one relationship or the other at risk.

It seemed to me that I was the one with the most at risk right this minute, though.

The sheriff walked me through the knot of people in the lobby too quickly for anyone to speak to me. He took me back to what I later learned was called the booking area. They took my fingerprints and a photograph, and I signed about a thousand different forms before the sheriff took me into the same interview room where we had talked before.

Hard to believe it had only been three days.

The sheriff set the recorder on the table without asking my permission. He stared at me, daring me to object. I didn't.

"Miss Neverall, I am going to talk to you for a few minutes, then you will be released.

Your mother has already arranged to post your bond, and Councilman Montgomery has spoken to me — quite eloquently, I might add — about your good character and reverence for the law.

"A reverence I have not seen expressed in your actions."

He sat forward and rested his thick fore-arms on the desk. I struggled to sit completely still in the uncomfortable metal chair. I felt like I was sliding forward, slightly off-balance, and I realized they must have changed the chairs before I came in. It wasn't the same chair as before.

I licked my lips, and caught the bottom one between my teeth. I would not chatter, no matter how nervous he made me.

"Now, you have been read your rights and you acknowledged that you understood them. Is that correct?"

He looked from me to the recorder.

I swallowed hard. "Yes."

"Do you remember what those rights were?"

Gulp. "Yes."

The sheriff took a deep breath and let it out. He talked in a slow voice, enunciating each word carefully, like he was talking to someone who didn't speak English well, or a very small child.

"Where did you go today?"

I chose my words carefully. "I went to see an old friend."

"That friend's name?"

"Richard Parks." I would answer his questions, but I wasn't going to say a single word that wasn't absolutely necessary. I'd seen enough cop shows to know that was how you got into trouble.

"Exactly where did you see this so-called old friend?"

"In Lucy's Diner."

The sheriff tensed. He flexed one hand, making a fist, relaxing the fingers, then squeezing it into a fist again.

"Where is Lucy's Diner located?"

"Near the corner of Sutter and Mason."

A corner of the sheriff's mouth twitched. He had gone past his initial annoyance to resignation. Although he fought the impulse to smile, I could see a flash of amusement.

"In what city, Miss Neverall?"

At least we were back to *Miss.* That was a good sign.

It was my turn not to smile as I answered. "San Francisco, Sheriff." The temptation to add *but you knew that* was strong and I had to bite the inside of my cheek to keep from saying it.

"And that is in California, is it not?"

"Yes."

The sheriff shook his head and leaned back. His leather chair with its ergonomically correct back support leaned with him, the leather creaking in the silence.

He shook his head. "Georgie, what part of 'don't leave town' didn't you understand?"

"You never said that."

"I told you not to plan any long trips. I thought you were smart enough to know what that meant."

I widened my eyes and tried to look innocent. I forced myself to look at him with a completely straight face. "I was only gone a few hours, Sheriff."

He wasn't amused by the answer or by my attempt to defend myself. "Which is exactly why you weren't picked up at the airport as soon as you landed in San Francisco," he answered. "You had booked a return flight and we had every reason to believe you would return.

"However, since you seem to need these things spelled out for you, here it is.

"You have been detained on a material witness warrant. You are not to leave the jurisdiction of this office without the permission of the court until this warrant is lifted. We believe you have information relating to the homicide of Blake Weston, and we want

279

you available for questioning in regards to that matter.

"We feel this action is necessary because you chose to leave the state in the middle of this investigation without telling anyone where you were going.

"Is this clear?"

"Yes, sir."

"That's all for now. We will expect you to be available for more questions at any time."

He turned off the recorder, and shot me a disgusted look. "That was about the dumbest move I have seen in a long time, Georgie. It looks damned suspicious to me, and I *know* you.

"Your mom is posting your bond. You should be free to go in a few minutes."

He gave me a long look. "Do. Not. Leave. Town."

He pushed his comfortable chair out the door, leaving me to sit in the sloped chair and wrap my arms around myself, trying to warm up, while I waited to be released.

Considering what was waiting for me outside, I probably should have been a little less anxious to leave.

In a few minutes a deputy came in with a stack of papers for me to sign. There was a copy of my original statement — the one I had never come back to sign — as well as several forms related to my detention. There was a bail form I signed, which said I would not leave the jurisdiction of the court without written permission. I had a hunch that was going to be really difficult to come by.

The bail receipt was the one that got me. My mother, the woman who didn't understand me and who I constantly disappointed, had pledged her house as a guarantee for my release.

When I finally walked out into the lobby my welcoming committee was milling around not knowing what to do with themselves. Mother and Gregory were sitting in a pair of the molded-plastic chairs, their heads close together.

Wade and Sue stood on opposite sides of the small room. From the thunderous expression on Sue's face, it had not been a pleasant wait.

As soon as I emerged, the race was on to see who could reach me first. Sue and Wade were practically body blocking one another, and in the confusion my mother got to me first.

She threw her arms around me and broke into sobs. I couldn't remember my mother crying. Ever. Even at my dad's funeral she had remained in control of her emotions;

though with the discoveries she had made in the days following Dad's death anger was a more likely expression than grief.

I was unnerved by this display. I found myself patting her on the back as she clung to me, reassuring her that everything was all right.

"But you were arrested," she wailed, a fresh burst of tears running down her face. Her makeup was already a ruin. As she dabbed ineffectively at her eyes she only succeeded in smudging the dark mascara into dark circles under them.

I managed to disengage Mother and deliver her into Gregory's waiting arms. She was still crying softly, but at least the worst of the storm had passed.

Wade and Sue were another story. Wade had wrapped his arm around my shoulders the instant my mother had released her death grip on me. Sue glared at him, and I turned to see a matching expression on his face.

"He could have waited until after dinner," Wade said. He was clearly continuing an earlier argument. "I would have brought her here myself."

"Sure. To protect your image." She moved in close to me, pointedly turning her body so that her back was to Wade. "Georgie, what did you think you were doing?"

"I was going to see an old friend. One that I thought might be able to give me some answers."

I looked over Sue's shoulder at Wade, then focused back on my best friend. "If the two of you can stop fighting over me like we were in the fifth grade, we can talk."

I lowered my voice, hoping Gregory was too preoccupied with my mother's tears to listen to me. "I think I know what happened. And why."

I raised my voice, pitching it to carry to my mother and Gregory. "Wade, could you take me to pick up my car, please? I'm really not hungry after all this, and I would just like to go home. I'm sure the dogs are anxious for a walk."

Sue leaned in close. "They're fine. I let them out a couple hours ago while we were waiting." She winked, and I knew she understood that I didn't want to talk in front of Gregory. Sue shared my opinion of the too-smooth Mr. Whitlock.

"Nonsense," my mother snapped. She had pulled herself together, and now she marched over and planted herself in front of me. "You'll come home, where I can take care of you."

That was more like the mom I knew.

"No, Mom. I have things I have to do at home. I need to be in my own house." I glanced behind her and caught a fleeting wave of relief pass across Gregory's face. He didn't want me in the house any more than I wanted to be there.

Besides, I needed to talk to Wade and Sue about the things I'd learned in San Francisco. And there was no way I could tell them what I knew with Mother around. Or Gregory.

"But you've just been arrested, Georgiana. And I posted your bail. I really think you should come home."

I took a deep breath. Mom was on my side, even though she had a peculiar way of showing it.

"I wasn't arrested. I haven't broken any law, and I haven't been charged with any crime."

Mom wasn't budging. "You had to post bail to get out of this dreadful place." She turned to Gregory, shaking her head. "I can hardly imagine a daughter of mine in a place like this."

She turned back to me. "And you left town when the sheriff said not to."

"That's not exactly what he said. But he's upset with me, and he wanted to be sure I

284

didn't do any more traveling without his say-so."

I looked back at Wade. "Can we blow this pop stand?"

"Georgiana! I want you to come home. After all, I did post your bail. I have a right to know where you are."

"You're welcome to stop by anytime to check on me, Mother, and I really do thank you for bailing me out." I could feel my temper rising and I worked to keep my voice down. "But I want to go home. *My* home. I have dogs that need to be taken care of, and I have a job to go to in the morning.

"If it's the money you're worried about," there was a trace of bitterness I couldn't hide, "I'll come in after my morning appointment and put the title of the 'Vette down in place of your house."

Mom took a step back. With her shocked expression and the circles of mascara under her eyes, she looked like a surprised raccoon. I managed not to giggle, though a bubble of hysterical laughter threatened to break free.

I fought down my growing panic, burying it beneath my remaining sliver of control. "I'm leaving," I said, walking toward the door. "I would appreciate a ride to my car, but I can walk if I have to."

It was a calculated bluff. After getting up before daylight to fly several hundred miles, tromping around San Francisco, and then coming home to the sheriff's dramatic gesture, I wasn't sure I could walk across the street.

But I would try if I had to.

Sue came to my rescue. "The SUV's in the front lot."

She held the door for me and tapped her remote. The lights flashed. Nothing had looked that good all day.

Wade ran to catch up with us. "I'll meet you at the house," he said and hurried past.

From behind us I heard a man's rapid footsteps. Gregory overtook us as I was climbing in Sue's SUV.

"Don't be too angry with her," he said. "She's just scared, and she doesn't handle it well. Sandy was really worried when the sheriff called looking for you.

"And don't worry about the money. We know you aren't going to do anything that would hurt her."

I nodded and climbed into the SUV. "Thanks."

"You will call her tomorrow, won't you, Georgie? She could use some reassurance that you really are okay."

"Yeah. I will." I didn't even cross my fingers.

CHAPTER 26

I buckled my seat belt with shaky fingers and leaned back against the headrest. The car held the distinct odor of dog. It was a comforting smell, reminding me of Daisy and Buddha, my two faithful companions.

My eyes closed and I relaxed for the first time all day. Sue was driving and I was safe for a few minutes.

"Georgie?" Sue shook my shoulder.

I jumped.

"Just resting my eyes," I said. I scrubbed my face with my palms, trying to scrape away the fog that had overtaken me. All I succeeded in doing was rubbing the faint traces of my early-morning makeup job into my eyes and making them water.

We were in Tiny's gravel parking lot, a couple spaces over from my car.

"You're in no shape to drive," Sue said. "We can come back for the Beetle in the morning."

I pulled my jacket tighter around me, trying to fight off the chill of fatigue that seeped into my bones. "You're right," I answered. The fog crept back over me.

I was forgetting something. Something important. "The laptop," I said as Sue reached to put the SUV in gear.

I patted my pockets until I found the key, climbed down from the SUV, and retrieved the case from the car. I relocked the doors, and gave the fender a pat. It really was safer in Tiny's lot overnight than it would be with me behind the wheel.

Wade was waiting in front of the house when we pulled up.

Once we were inside and the dogs were outside — the rugs were amazingly still intact — I confronted the two people I was closest to.

"If you two are going to argue," I said, putting as much force as I could muster behind my words, "then you might as well leave right this minute.

"I'm fine, I am not in any real trouble with the law, and I am not going to have you two making a big deal out of this. There are a lot more important things to talk about.

"Got it?"

Sue looked like she was about to protest, and I gave her my sternest look. She closed her mouth and nodded.

I looked at Wade, waiting for his agreement. He was hesitating.

"Have I got this right?" I asked. "My boyfriend is fighting with my best friend because *her* boyfriend did his job? Is that about it?"

Wade winced at my blunt description, because it was accurate.

Sue colored a little, muttering, "He's not my boyfriend."

"Beside the point." I cut her off. "I broke up with you once" — I looked at Wade — "because I thought I had to choose."

I looked back to Sue. "And I am not doing it again because of your boyfriend. We all know how well that worked out the first time."

"Not my boyfriend."

"Yeah? And why do you blush every time somebody mentions him? And call him Fred while the rest of us call him Sheriff? He *so* is your boyfriend.

"But that isn't what I wanted to talk about. You guys get that, right?"

They both nodded. A bit sullenly, but I really didn't care, as long as I had their cooperation.

I thought about the microbrew in the refrigerator, but rejected it in favor of hot chocolate. I puttered around the kitchen, while Sue let the dogs in and gave them their treats.

With the cocoa in steaming mugs, I led the way into the living room and pointed to chairs.

"Sit."

Buddha, ever obedient, plopped his behind down next to my feet and looked at me expectantly. Following commands required a treat in his world.

Sue tried to stifle a giggle, but she failed. Wade grinned and the two of them leaned back in their chairs. We had a truce, thanks to Buddha.

He got his treat.

"I need your help, guys. I think I know who killed Blake, and I think I know why. But I can't prove it."

Wade's brow furrowed with worry.

"I'll make this quick, I promise," I said. "Just don't interrupt."

I ran down the information I had gathered. Whitlock needed money, and so did Samurai, and it looked like Samurai had the inside track with McComb. What I didn't know was just how desperate Gregory's financial situation was.

I looked at Wade, and he shook his head. "We've had this talk before, Georgie. I can't reveal anything about my clients' finances. You know that."

I nodded. "So it's that bad."

"What? He didn't say anything." Sue looked puzzled.

"Exactly. Which is what I expected. See, if it wasn't bad, he'd have said I was wrong, or I didn't know anything, or something like that. Instead he said he can't tell me anything.

"Which tells me I'm right. Gregory Whitlock is in serious financial trouble."

"But that doesn't make him a murderer," Sue protested.

"No, it doesn't. But it gives him a motive. And who else is there? Besides me, I mean."

No one had an answer for that.

"There's something else," I said. I told them about the rest of my conversation with Richard, about Blake wanting to talk me into coming back to Samurai and about the buyout rumors.

"So Blake was angry with me. It explains a lot about how he acted." I paused and shook my head. "But it could all have been cleared up if he'd just talked to me."

"I'm trying to work up some sympathy for him on that score," Wade said. "But it sounds like he was pretty quick to believe some nasty rumors about you, so it's kind of difficult.

"But I have to ask, Georgie. What are you going to do?"

That was the million-dollar question. The one I didn't have an answer for.

I shrugged. "I wish I knew. I don't think the sheriff really believes I killed Blake, even if Daisy and Buddha" — the Airedales wagged their tails at the mention of their names — "can't support my alibi."

"He doesn't," Sue said. "Just that when you ran off like that he didn't have much choice."

"I know. And I'm sorry I put him on the spot like that. But I had to talk to somebody at Samurai, and Richard was my best bet.

"And, to tell the truth, I was afraid he wouldn't talk to me on the phone. Flying down there was the only way I could be sure he'd tell me what I needed to know."

"But that's beside the point," Wade dragged the discussion back to his question. "What are you going to do?"

I shook my head. "I have to go do the evaluation with Chad McComb and Stan Fischer in the morning. Maybe that will give me some idea. Because right now, I haven't got a clue."

Sue and Wade both tried to come up with some other explanation for Blake's death. I had to admit, it was possible it had nothing to do with Samurai, or Chad McComb, or anything we knew about. But I didn't believe it. Why else was he killed here in Pine Ridge?

"What if it's someone from your old company?" Sue asked. "Maybe there was a power struggle within the company and someone wanted him out of the way."

"I thought of that. But from the way Richard and Stan both talked I had the feeling Blake was the one holding the company together. Richard was better technically than Blake. Heck, he was better than me. But he was right about the clients.

"Richard doesn't do that whole meet-and-greet thing, and he was never a salesman. Blake had the self-confidence and the charm to do both."

He was certainly able to sell me, I added silently. I still didn't believe Richard's defense of Blake.

"In that case," Wade said slowly, "what if someone from outside the company wanted to take over? With Blake out of the way, they might have a golden opportunity."

I shook my head. "Blake was running the show. Without him, there wasn't that much to take over, I don't think. Just some technical talent, and they could be hired away.

They wouldn't have to kill Blake for that."

My predawn drive to the airport caught up with me. I yawned so wide I felt like my jaw would crack open.

My eyelids were drooping, and I needed to sleep. I had to be at my best for the meeting with Chad McComb and Stan Fischer in the morning at the McComb job site.

The Beetle was still sitting in Tiny's parking lot, and I didn't want to take the 'Vette out to the site. The mud and potholes of the access road were too unforgiving for my garage queen.

With a sigh I dragged my cell phone from my pocket. Stan's hotel number was in the call log, and I punched up the number while I explained the situation to Wade and Sue.

They offered to go pick up the car, but I turned them down. Stan could pick me up, and he or Chad could drop me back in town after our meeting. There was no reason to put my friends out any more than they already were.

Besides, I didn't trust anyone else with the Beetle's aging automatic stick shift. Not many people knew how to operate one, and I didn't want to try and explain it.

Stan answered and we made arrangements for him to pick me up at the house in the morning.

A few minutes later I shooed Wade and Sue out the door, with a promise that I wouldn't do anything foolish without talking to them first.

It was an easy promise to make. I wasn't likely to do anything foolish in bed, sound asleep.

CHAPTER 27

There was much to be said for riding in Stan's rented Lincoln. For starters, the heater worked. The Beetle heater was marginal at best, and some days it didn't actually warm up until I'd reached my destination.

"I owe you an apology, Georgie Girl," Stan said as we cruised out of town on the highway. "I'm afraid I might have spilled the beans about you and Blake to the sheriff.

"I didn't mean to," he said, glancing at me then turning his gaze back to the road. "But when I told him you two had been pretty serious he was mighty interested."

He glanced back at me again, but I kept my eyes straight ahead. He couldn't have told the sheriff anything I hadn't already divulged. He didn't know anything else to tell.

"Course I told him it was all ancient history, and Blake had a couple girlfriends since then. Moved on and all that."

This was news to me. Richard hadn't said anything about another girlfriend. If anything, he had implied that Blake still carried the torch for months after I left. I wondered why the two men had such different opinions of Blake's reaction. Maybe because Richard projected his feelings onto Blake?

"It's not a problem, Stan. I'd already told him about Blake and me."

I guided Stan through the tangle of unmarked roads that wandered through the undeveloped area outside Pine Ridge and led to the McComb site. The Lincoln glided up the final grade with minimal effort from the hefty V-8 under the hood.

Chad McComb's Range Rover was already parked in the gravel lot at the top of the grade. We climbed out of the car and walked over to where Chad stood surveying the abandoned-looking construction site.

A shiver passed over me as I realized no one had been back to the site since Blake Weston had been killed. Work stopped the night before Blake's death, and had never resumed.

Chad greeted Stan and me. He didn't ask, but I could see the question in his eyes. What was one of the plumbers doing out here with his security consultant?

Stan caught the look, too. "Mr. McComb, I'd like you to meet Georgiana Neverall."

Chad looked puzzled. "I know Georgie. She's been working on this project since the beginning. Barry Hickey says she's one of his best workers."

"Ah, yes." Stan grinned. "You know Georgie, the plumber. But do you know Georgiana, the security expert?"

Chad shot me a look, and I felt the color climb up my neck and spread across my face. Chad's eyes widened.

"I used to work for Stan, before I moved back to Pine Ridge," I acknowledged, hoping Stan would let me leave it at that.

"One of the best in the business," Stan said expansively. "I'm trying to convince her to come back. She may be a good worker for Mr. Hickey, but she's wasting her talent digging ditches." He nodded toward the moat. "She's promised to help with the initial appraisal, at least until I can get a replacement up here for Mr. Weston."

Chad glanced at the moat when Stan mentioned Blake's name. "My condolences again on your loss, Mr. Fischer. And you, Georgie. You knew him, didn't you? I remember him talking to you in Tiny's that first night he was here.

"I'm so sorry for your loss."

"We worked together a long time ago," I said. I smiled to soften the words, and quickly moved away from the topic of the late Mr. Weston.

"Tell me about the plans, Mr. McComb."

"Georgie, it's Chad, remember?"

I nodded. "I've seen some of the plans, and I managed to look over the few notes Mr. Weston had already provided to Stan. But why don't you tell me what you're looking for?"

Just as I expected, Chad McComb had plans for an elaborate computer installation. The entire castle would be wired for high-speed Internet access, there were redundant backup systems, and a direct line to his old employer for especially sensitive data.

"So, not completely retired, huh?" I teased.

Chad colored, but he smiled sheepishly. "It's hard to let go," he said. "I love what I do — did — and they still ask for my advice now and then. Lets me keep a finger in the pie, so to speak."

"I know what you mean, McComb," Stan boomed. "They put me on the board of directors, but I still get an itch to get my hands dirty."

"I'm going to take a look around." I

glanced at Chad. "Just to get a feel for how this fits in with the rest of the project. I'm familiar with some of it, but I'd like a little time to study the site."

Stan waved a hand at me. "Go on, look at whatever it is you need to. I'll just have me a little talk with Chad here about the details of the contract."

I was obviously dismissed while the two men talked about money. I knew from Richard that Stan and Samurai were looking for more than a single contract. They were looking for an open checkbook and deep pockets to solve their cash flow problem.

I silently wished Stan luck and strolled away, notebook in hand, to scout the site. From the way he focused his attention on Chad, it was clear he was the big fish Richard had been talking about.

It took me the better part of an hour to walk the site and make note of the things we would need to do for the security installation. Just like the other utilities, several access cables would need to come in under the moat.

It looked like I would have to dig up the moat, again, to bury more conduit. I sighed. Why couldn't they get this organized so we could do it once and be done with it?

Each time I stopped to make a note, I

glanced back to Chad and Stan. The two stood in the middle of what would eventually be the central courtyard, and Chad was talking animatedly, often gesturing with sweeping movements of his arms.

I had seen him like this on other occasions, when he'd come to the site with a visitor. He was describing the castle for Stan, who listened with a big show of interest.

I was sure Stan didn't give a hoot about Chad's castle. But he'd be as interested and impressed as he had to be to get at Chad's checkbook.

It was why he was here instead of Richard, or one of the other tech guys. And it was why I was here getting a handsome consulting fee to do the real work of laying out the system.

I remembered the credit card bill that would show up soon, and went back to making notes.

A week ago I had watched Blake walking around the site with Chad, and thought that this was a job I would have done in a heartbeat. And now I was doing the job, falling right back into the routines and procedures that had made me, as Stan said, one of the best.

Did I miss this? Was I fooling myself that

I wanted to be a plumber? I was already designing the system in my head even though I knew I would have to catch up on current technology. I was configuring hardware and applications that would safeguard the data Chad would pipe into the castle — and I was enjoying it.

Was I getting sucked back into the life I swore I'd left behind? More important, did I want to get sucked back in?

I brushed aside the questions. For now, I was simply earning my fee. Nothing more.

I was a plumber. An apprentice, granted, but the time was coming when I would take my exams and have my certification. This was my new life, and it was where I belonged.

I rejoined Stan and Chad McComb. Stan didn't look happy.

Chad McComb hadn't become rich by being a pushover. Sure he'd been in the right place, in the right industry, at just the right time. But he was no one's fool, and it looked like Stan had underestimated just how shrewd Chad could be.

It must have been an interesting conversation.

Stan was preoccupied on the ride back to town, and I left him alone with his thoughts. I had plenty of my own to worry about.

I gave him directions back to town, though he didn't seem to need them. I had never actually ridden with him before, and I was impressed with his recall of the route — he didn't even glance at the fancy GPS system. Occasionally he would confirm a turn before he made it, but I could tell he didn't need to.

When he pulled into the lot at Tiny's he suggested we have lunch at Dee's, but I declined. "I need to get these notes together for whoever is taking over the project, Stan. You will have someone up here soon, won't you?"

He shook his head. "Are you sure you won't do it, Georgie? I really could use you."

"I'm sure." I opened the door and fished the key to the Beetle out of my pocket.

I wasn't having this conversation again. With anyone. Tomorrow morning I would be back in the bottom of the moat, putting in another piece of conduit for the security system. I could hardly wait to hear Barry's reaction when I told him we'd have to dig again. He'd be almost as happy as I was.

"Georgie?"

"Not a chance, Stan."

I closed the door on Stan and his pleas.

The Beetle was cold, and it took a few minutes to clear the windshield enough to drive. My stomach growled and I glanced at my watch. It was only a little after eleven, but maybe I could persuade Wade to take an early lunch.

I drove the few blocks to Wade's office, hunched over the steering wheel so I could see out of the mostly clear portion of the windshield closest to the defroster vent.

Wade was at his desk, papers spread across the credenza behind him. A fat book was open on the side of the desk, and he was making notes on a pad in front of him.

A smile spread across his face when I walked in. "Hi, beautiful."

"Hi, yourself. You have time for an early lunch?"

He glanced up at the clock. "In a couple minutes. Just let me finish checking this tax citation."

He went back to his book without waiting for an answer.

I sat for a few seconds in his visitor chair, but was soon on my feet, prowling the office. There was a second desk where his secretary used to work. She had quit a couple years ago to get married and move to Omaha, and he had never missed her enough to replace her.

I sat at the desk and opened my laptop. I

could begin organizing my notes while I was waiting.

The laptop booted, and flashed a message. "Wireless network available."

Curious, I launched the wireless connection screen. There were a couple of networks within range.

One of them was Wade's office LAN. He didn't need a network, since there was only one computer in the office, as far as I knew. But there it was, waiting for me to click on the icon and connect to the files that held all the financial information for Whitlock Estates. And Gregory. And my mother.

All there for the taking.

I clicked on the connection, and was relieved to see that at least it was password-protected. It wasn't just open for anyone with a wireless card to tap into.

But I was a computer security expert, and even though I was rusty I was sure I could defeat the relatively unsophisticated level of protection that would be on Wade's system.

After all, I had designed and installed systems for companies with really sensitive data. The kind that required men in dark suits and thin ties to check you out before they let you work.

Wade's system wouldn't even be a challenge. I tried to ignore the uncomfortable knowledge that Wade's system was only accessible because he trusted me, and forged ahead.

I fiddled for a few minutes, digging into places in the system that most people didn't know existed.

It was nothing more than old tricks I had learned over the years. Some dated back to college, and I had learned more in the early years at Samurai. It always impressed a prospective client when I sat down and accessed their date files in a matter of minutes.

Those tricks won us a lot of contracts.

I tracked through logs and files, unlocking encrypted information and digging deeper with each passing minute. I told myself I was only trying to protect myself and my mother, that I needed to know the truth about Mom and Gregory's financial dealings.

Wade flipped a page, and muttered to himself. I glanced at him, ready to slam the laptop closed if he came my direction, but he was immersed in the reference book.

He didn't pay any attention to what I was doing.

My heart raced and my palms grew damp against the keyboard.

Computer passwords were a balancing act between something the user could easily remember and something an intruder would be unable to guess. Most passwords didn't take long to guess, and I knew several ways to discover at least a few characters. From there, it was usually easy to fill in the rest.

Computer security was a lot like plumbing. You designed and built a system to allow water — or data — to only flow in one direction. Sometimes you wanted the outside world to send data to you, just like your incoming water pipe. And sometimes you wanted to only allow outgoing transfers, like the wastewater system. The whole point of the security system was to control what direction that data flowed.

Wade's system was designed to take data in. There were access points for his clients to connect to his system and send him their information — sales, expenses, payroll — all the details he collected in order to tell them if they were making money, or owed taxes, or whatever else he advised them about.

What I wanted to do was get into his system and draw the information out. Sort of like in the movies when the robbers get into the building by crawling through the sewer pipes.

I had never seen an outlet pipe that was actually big enough for a man to crawl through, but in the make-believe world of spy movies it looked cool and that was all that mattered.

I pulled my attention back to the task at hand. I might have only a few minutes more before Wade was finished and ready for lunch.

A few characters emerged, and a pattern began to form. People were creatures of habit. You could always find a pattern. And this wasn't just anyone. It was Wade, a man I knew well. Someone I had known for a long time. A man who trusted me. I shoved the thought aside.

I heard Wade's chair creak, and I swiveled to look at him. My hand was poised on the laptop, ready to snap it shut before he could see what I was doing.

"About ready," he said. "Just let me clean up a little." He pushed back from the desk and walked past the door of the tiny private consultation room to the washroom in the back of the office.

I had a couple minutes reprieve, but he would be back soon.

I listened for the running water that would signal his imminent return, as my fingers flew across the keyboard.

Just a few more characters to go.

I looked in horror at the words that

emerged.

It was a phrase I remembered well.

"Georgie Nevermore."

It was the juvenile play on my name I had used the day I broke up with him over Sue's cheating boyfriend. It was how I told him to think of me when I had given him my self-righteous speech about friendship and loyalty and trust.

I closed the window and broke the connection. I could find some other way to get the information I needed.

A way that didn't violate Wade's trust in me.

CHAPTER 28

I barely remembered lunch. I know I talked to Wade and he talked to me, but I couldn't stop obsessing about the mistake I had almost made. I had been drawn back into the world I'd left behind and very nearly betrayed the trust of one of my best friends.

The dogs greeted me enthusiastically when I returned home. They wanted a walk, but I didn't want to be alone with my thoughts for that long.

I needed a distraction.

My *gi* was in the closet of the second bedroom.

I began my routine, concentrating on the precision of my movements, the control of my body, and the focus of my breathing. Slowly, I felt my concerns drain away as I reached down inside me for calm and control.

I wished again for a dojo and a sensei, then realized I no longer needed them. I used my martial arts training to gain control over my temper and negative emotions, and I had learned to do that on my own. I had gained the control I needed without anyone's help.

It was a wonderful feeling.

Stress never solved a problem, it only made it worse. Although I had regained control, I still desperately needed a solution.

The key had to be Gregory's finances. If he was in serious trouble, he could have been desperate enough to try and stop Blake.

I had stopped myself from snooping in Wade's computer, but there was another place to look. Gregory's files. I could break into the files of Whitlock Estates Realty.

I would be doing the exact thing I had battled against for all my years at Samurai. The same thing I had nearly done to Wade. The difference was I didn't trust Gregory, and I didn't think he trusted me.

It had nothing to do with his relationship with my mother. I had to save my own skin. The sheriff hadn't arrested me for murder, and he still acted as though he believed I was innocent. But how long would that last if I didn't find out who really did do it? How long before I *was* arrested and charged with

Blake's murder?

As Barbara Parks had said, it didn't look good.

Desperate times call for desperate measures. And although I had mastered my rising panic, I was still in a desperate situation and it was time to act.

My desktop whirred to life, and I began tapping keys. There was a public website for Whitlock Estates. I would start there.

A long, frustrating hour later I had found the hosting system for the website, but there was no link back to the Whitlock computers.

Strike one.

It had been a long shot, after all. I hadn't really expected it to be that easy, had I?

I went back to work, trying another avenue. Perhaps I could find information in public records that would tell me about the status of Whitlock Estates. I spent the entire afternoon crawling through search after search, combing public records, news archives, blog posts, anywhere I could find a mention of Whitlock or Clackamas Commons. I didn't find anything that indicated whether Whitlock and the Commons were solvent or not.

I turned up a couple public-record filings that weren't supposed to be searchable.

Clackamas Commons was incorporated, and the named officers were Gregory, my mother, and the attorney who had filed the incorporation. Fortunately for Mom it wasn't either of the Gladstones, who were in jail awaiting trial for the murder of Martha Tepper.

Beyond that there was nothing.

Strike two.

The sun had set and outside the night was quickly turning cold. There was a hint of winter in the air; snow and ice would soon keep most of Pine Ridge indoors.

I hoped we would be able to finish the McComb project before the weather shut us down for the winter. It didn't matter how much of a premium Chad McComb was willing to pay, there were times when you just couldn't work outside.

I shut down the computer, fed the dogs, and changed into the warmest clothes I could find. The morning's visit to Wade's office had given me an idea. I had my doubts whether it would work, but it was the only other thing I could think of.

The parking lot at the back of the Whitlock Estates office was deserted. A streetlight in front of the office cast a dark shadow over the lot, perfect for my purposes.

I parked close to the building, putting the

Beetle deep in the shadow. When I opened the laptop the glow of the screen seemed overly bright in the darkness. I adjusted the display until I could just make out what I was doing on the dimly lit screen and set to work.

I scanned for available networks, and found several. I shook my head at the trusting folks of Pine Ridge. There were at least two local businesses whose networks were not only visible but open and unprotected. I could have prowled through their records and stolen their data if I wanted to.

Pine Ridge needed serious education about computer security. I hoped Gregory Whitlock was as clueless as the rest of the business owners.

I worked my way down the list of available networks, discarding the ones I could identify. Some names were obvious, and some were more obscure. I came to a network named *Commonsnet,* and my heart quickened. Commonsnet — for Clackamas Commons, perhaps? But no, it was a network for libertarian politicians, "in honor of the common man."

I moved on.

Out on the street a car passed, its headlights cutting through the shadows. I lowered the screen of the laptop, shielding the glow from the display. Once the car was gone I waited, breathing shallowly, to see if it would return. When it didn't I went back to work.

I discarded several more networks before I hit pay dirt. It wasn't actually a network, just an unsecured computer left running. A few minutes of digging revealed it to be a "visitor" computer on the Whitlock network.

I was about to connect to the computer when my cell phone buzzed. I had set it on vibrate to keep it silent, but the hum of the instrument against my thigh made my heart race.

I glanced at the tiny screen. It was Stan Fischer, calling from his hotel.

I knew the parking lot was deserted, but I looked around anyway. There was no one to hear me.

"Hello?"

"Georgie Girl," Stan's voice boomed from the phone. I frantically thumbed the volume control. "I'm heading for the airport in a couple minutes, girl. Gotta get back and arrange to get somebody up here. Unless" — I could hear the sly smile in his voice — "you've changed your mind about takin' the job."

"No, Stan. Can't do it."

Stan sighed dramatically. "If you're absolutely sure, then I guess I have to try and take no for an answer — and you know how hard that is for me."

He chuckled, and I felt the corners of my mouth lift in an answering grin. It was a good thing he couldn't see me, he might take it as a sign I was weakening, and maybe I was. But the force of Stan's personality wasn't quite as strong over the phone as it was in person. Lucky for me.

"Will you send me your notes?" he asked. He rattled off an e-mail address I knew I could easily remember: S Fischer at Samurai Security. The domain I used to own, when I still owned Samurai Security itself.

"Be glad to, Stan."

"Okay then. Maybe I'll get back up here sometime soon, check in on the job and all that."

Check in on Chad McComb's checkbook, more likely. But at least he would keep Samurai operating. It might not be my company anymore, but to my surprise I found I still wanted it to succeed.

I got Stan off the phone, and stowed it in my jacket pocket. Then I went back to the Whitlock network.

I established a connection with the "visitor" computer, and roamed through the system until I found the link to the Whit-

317

lock network controller. The computer I was talking to didn't have permission to access most of Whitlock's files. Which meant I had to spend a few minutes manipulating the network security to change that.

Finally, with access to the network I edited the password files, allowing my laptop to reach everything on the network.

I clicked quickly through the files, looking for anything that might be significant. I downloaded one file after another, copying them to a folder on my laptop.

The phone buzzed again, but this time I ignored it. I would worry about who it was later. Right now I was grabbing everything I could off of Gregory's computer.

The files took several minutes to copy. All the while I waited in the dark car, barely daring to breathe for fear someone would notice me.

Pine Ridge is a small town, and most everything closes early. Still, an irrational fear gripped me as I sat there, watching the progress bar slowly tick across the screen.

I silently urged it to go faster. My hands clenched into fists and my shoulders drew tighter and tighter.

I felt a muscle spasm run down one leg and fought to hold down the surprised yelp of pain that rose in my throat.

I reached deep inside, pulling myself back under control, focusing on breathing properly. I stretched the cramping leg as best I could in the tight confines of the Beetle, and concentrated on forcing the muscle to stretch out and relax.

The pain slowly subsided.

I drew a deep, ragged breath as I regained control of my racing heartbeat.

The files had only a few seconds to run.

As soon as they finished downloading, I covered my electronic tracks, slammed the laptop closed, and started the Beetle's engine.

I left the lights off as I drove between the Whitlock office and the building next door. I reached the street and looked both ways. The street was empty.

I turned on the lights, pulled out into the street, and headed home. I had a long night ahead of me, digging through the masses of data I had just hijacked from Gregory's computer.

And we were going back to work on the moat first thing tomorrow morning.

I sighed. Sleep was for wimps.

CHAPTER 29

I rubbed my burning eyes and rolled my aching shoulders in small circles. The kitchen window glowed a dark gray with the hint of sunrise. Daisy roused herself from her bed in the corner of the living room and padded in to where I sat at the kitchen table.

She laid her head in my lap, offering comfort and begging to be petted at the same time. I scratched her behind the ears, feeling her wiry coat beneath my hand.

The notepad on the table next to me held several pages of notes, scribbles, questions, and impromptu math problems. As near as I could tell, Gregory Whitlock was deeply in debt and his situation had been deteriorating for several months.

Simply put, based on the files I'd downloaded — I couldn't bring myself to admit I had stolen them — Gregory was on the verge of bankruptcy.

If he could hang on a few months, which

wasn't likely from what I saw, the completion of Clackamas Commons might bail him out. It still wouldn't restore his financial health, but it would get him off life support.

Bankruptcy would be a harsh prospect for Gregory. He was in an industry where image meant at least as much as substance. The specter of reorganization — even a successful one — would threaten his livelihood as well as his self-image.

That just might make him desperate enough to kill.

I let out the dogs and staggered into the shower. I let the hot water run over my body, then slowly cooled the spray until the frigid water shocked me into a semblance of consciousness.

I was tired, but I'd pulled all-nighters before and I could do it again.

The sun still hadn't made its appearance when I started the Beetle. I was early for work, but I could pick up a mocha on the way. The caffeine and sugar would give me a little boost to start the morning and I had an insulated carafe of coffee to keep me going through the day.

One problem with driving an older car: no cup holders. I balanced the steaming mocha against my thigh as I made my way through the woods to the McComb site.

A faint line of gold traced the horizon when I pulled into the gravel lot. The surrounding woods were quiet, the silence broken by the occasional call of an early-morning bird, or the rustle of a squirrel.

I leaned against the fender of the Beetle and sipped at the mocha. The beauty of the site washed over me as I stood there, surrounded by tall evergreens and the riotously colored oaks and vine maple.

I was going to have to decide what to do about Mom and Gregory. What was I going to tell her?

I knew the answer. I couldn't divulge what I knew without telling her how I found out, and I wasn't ready to do that. But what I could do, what I knew I *would* do, was tell her the truth about me and about Blake.

After work, before I lost my nerve, I would go see her and confess my failures. Mom was too trusting, but she wasn't stupid. She had to know what Gregory's financial situation was. She was too deeply involved not to. She would see the parallels between Blake and Gregory, and draw her own conclusion.

The thought of admitting to her how stupid I had been turned my stomach sour. Humiliation, even voluntary humiliation, wasn't something I looked forward to.

But she had put her house on the line for me, and I would do whatever it took to protect my mother. She had already nearly lost everything because of one man — because my father was too soft-hearted to ask his patients to pay him.

I couldn't let her lose everything again.

The line of gold on the horizon dimmed as storm clouds moved in. The weather report had called for overcast, but no rain. From the look of the clouds, they were probably wrong.

In the distance I heard a powerful engine laboring up the climb to the job site. It was still early for the crew, and it didn't sound like Barry's monster diesel. Someone was climbing the road to the site of Chad Mc-Comb's castle.

With the weather closing in, we'd all end up turning around and going home. Maybe it was Sean, coming out to be sure we all got the message.

A purring Lincoln climbed the rise and pulled into the gravel lot near the Beetle. I was surprised to see Stan's rental car. Hadn't he said he was flying back to San Francisco last night?

Stan wasn't alone. Maybe he had flown down to meet Blake's replacement and come back to smooth the introductions with

Chad McComb. It would be a sensible move if he wanted to work his way into Chad's good graces, and his deep pockets.

"Figured I'd find you up here, Georgie Girl. I know how you like to get to the job earlier than everybody else."

My answering chuckle died in my throat. Barbara Parks climbed out of the passenger side of the Lincoln.

She was dressed in jeans and a sweatshirt, loafers on her feet, and a scarf tossed elegantly around her throat. Without Richard beside her, her height was impressive. I hadn't realized before what an imposing woman she was.

"Barbara. I didn't expect to see you. Is everything all right?"

"I certainly hope so," Stan said. Although the morning was chilly, sweat stood out on his forehead. "But there are some things we need to talk about." He cleared his throat, a nervous sound I would have never expected from Stan Fischer. "We thought this would be a good time to talk to you. Alone."

The last word hung in the air, an ominous sound.

He was right. I was alone. Completely. No one was due at the site for at least another half hour. My lizard brain tried to take over, telling me to run away.

"I didn't realize you two knew each other," I said. "But I guess it makes sense, since Barbara's husband works for you."

Barbara glared at me, and I wondered what I'd said wrong. She was quick to correct me.

"Stanley should be working for him. Richard is the best thing that company has going for it."

I nodded. "That's what I tried to tell him. Stan, I mean. Richard's one of the best. Better than I was."

"That's for sure," she said. Her voice dripped condescension. "He says you were good." She shrugged. "Maybe you *were*, but he's better, and he knows what he's doing. There is no way they should bring you back into the company."

I looked at Stan. He wouldn't meet my gaze, looking out over the trees as though I wasn't there.

"That's what I told Stan. Isn't it, Stan? I told you to bring Richard up here, that he should be doing this job."

"She did say that." Stan moved a few steps away, distancing himself from the growing confrontation. "Told me she wouldn't take the job."

"Right." Barbara didn't believe a word either of us was saying. "Then why did she come all the way down to San Francisco? To talk about dear, departed Blake? The Blake she abandoned when she ran away?"

Anger washed over me. "You don't know anything about Blake and me!"

"I know what he told me. I know he refused to get serious about our relationship because he still had some crazy idea that you'd come back some day."

Stan walked back and stood next to Barbara. He put a hand on her arm, rubbing and patting as though trying to soothe a petulant child.

"That doesn't matter anymore, Barb. That was a long time ago. You have Richard now, right?"

"And all I've heard for the last two days is Georgie-this and Georgie-that. I'm sick of it already, and it's going to get worse. A lot worse." Her voice rose with each sentence, anger and resentment growing with each word.

"Barbara!" Stan shook the arm he'd been patting as he spoke her name sharply. "This isn't about your personal problems. This is about Samurai, and what's best for the company."

Stan looked over at me and tried to turn on the charm. Did I mention he didn't have any?

"Georgie Girl. We need your help. Samurai is having some little problems. Just a hiccup or two, really. But we need to keep everything on an even keel for a few weeks. That's all."

His wheedling tone brought back memories of another early-morning meeting. One where he'd invoked the same argument: what was best for Samurai.

The morning he claimed what was best was my resignation.

The lizard brain was screaming now. Something was definitely wrong. I forced myself to remain calm and asked levelly, "What can I do for you, Stan?"

He smiled, relief evident as his posture relaxed. "It's about those buyout rumors. I know they're wrong, you know they're wrong. But the people back at Samurai, they don't know it, and it would upset a lot of people if that came out right now. Besides" — I could almost see the wheels turning in his head as he continued — "there *could* be a buyout. Just a little bit late.

"Help us through this, Georgie Girl, and I can see to it that a settlement comes your way when we're back on track."

I looked from Stan to Barbara, trying to figure out the connection. "Okay," I said. "But what does she have to do with all this?

Why is she even here?"

"I needed a witness," he lied. "I didn't want anyone from Samurai involved, and Barbara was the only other person who knew you. I didn't think you'd want to talk about this in front of a stranger, would you?"

"So," I said slowly, "I tell Richard the rumors were true, everybody goes back to normal, you get the money you need from Chad, and we all live happily ever after?"

"See?" Stan beamed at Barbara. "I told you she was a smart girl."

She shook her head. "It won't work, Stan. She wanted Blake back, and look what happened. Pretty soon she'll want Richard back. I can't let that happen, Stan. I have too much invested in him."

"Oh, c'mon," Stan joshed. "You have to be able to cut your losses. I've done it a lot. Just pay what you have to and walk away." He looked over at me. "That's what we'll do here, won't we, Georgie? We'll all walk away."

He chuckled to himself, though I didn't see anything remotely amusing about the situation. I was trapped on the top of a hill, miles from anyone, with a couple of crazy people who thought they could bribe me to cover up — what, exactly?

"What I don't understand, Stan, is where

those rumors came from, anyway. How did everyone get the idea I took an offer and walked away?"

His smug grin answered my question before his words. Now that he thought I'd accepted his plan, he wanted to let me know how clever he'd been. "Must have been Blake," he said slyly. "After I told him you were leaving. And why."

My stomach hollowed and I fought back the impulse to gag. "And that was when, Stan? The night before I talked to you?"

He nodded. "I was real sorry about it, too. But I tried to tell you two that an office romance wasn't a good idea. You didn't leave me much choice.

"You got to him, Georgie. He told me he was going to back your demands to the board. Couldn't have the two of you doing that, so I did what I had to do."

Barbara watched me, her face intense. I breathed deeply. I had to look calm, feel calm. Stan had fooled himself into believing I was on board with the plan, but she wasn't as easily fooled.

Stan turned down the corners of his mouth, a mockery of real human emotion. "It hurt me, Georgie. It really did. I knew it wasn't going to last anyway, but I'd have rather let you two find that out on your own." He shook his head sadly.

"I know it hurt you both, but you got over it. I hear you have a new man in your life. So there was no real harm, was there?"

I shrugged my shoulders, and waved away his comment as though it didn't matter. I didn't want to argue with either Stan or Barbara while I was here alone. If I could stall a few minutes longer, someone was sure to arrive.

A fat raindrop hit my outstretched hand, mocking my confidence in the cavalry coming to my rescue. Instead of coming out to the site, Sean and Barry were probably calling everyone and reassigning them.

Nobody was coming to save me.

Barbara clutched her leather bag against her side, shielding it from the rain. She looked like she wanted to climb back into the shelter of the Lincoln, but she wouldn't let me out of her sight.

"But why a buyout, Stan?" I stalled. "You guys had the authority to fire me. Why not just do it?"

"You had friends in the company. We couldn't risk you talking to them, telling them what really happened. Once they were convinced you'd walked away, we would be safe.

"And if you were right — which you

were," the admission made him grimace, "we were covered. Nobody could blame the board if you quit and walked away with a chunk of money. We were even able to spin the buyout as part of the cash flow problem.

"Everybody wins."

Except me.

The rain came down harder. Barbara clutched her bag to her chest like a shield.

"Blake was going to ruin everything," Barbara interjected. "He was going to ask you to come back, to take your old job back. Take back your company. Your job. Blake. Richard. You were going to take everything."

She reached in her bag, and there was a terrifying moment of déjà vu. Seconds later I was staring at the barrel of a gun.

Stan backed away from her toward the door of the Lincoln. "We agreed, Barbara. We can trust Georgie. We can make a deal. You heard her." His eyes pleaded with me to back him up. "She's on board with our plans."

She spoke to Stan from the corner of her mouth. "You can tell yourself whatever you want, Stanley, but you know better. She was going to ruin everything, just like Blake was. You know it was only a matter of how long before we had to get rid of her.

"I came prepared this time."

This time? Which meant what? That she'd been here before? And if she wasn't prepared the last time?

She'd used whatever was at hand. Something hard and heavy.

She was a big woman. Tall and well muscled. She could easily hit a man hard enough to knock him down.

Break his ribs.

Inflict serious injuries.

Kill him.

Chapter 30

Everybody moved at once.

Stan dove for the car door and shoved himself behind the wheel of the big Lincoln.

Barbara dropped her bag in the mud and took a step toward me, the gun raised.

The lizard brain seized control, and I ran. It didn't matter where; I just had to get away.

Behind me I heard the roar of the Lincoln's massive engine and the spinning of wheels as the big car fought for traction in the gravel.

Bits of rock whizzed past me, shot from under the tires. Seconds later a final spray of gravel signaled the tires grabbing the surface. The engine sound roared down the hill behind me. I didn't bother looking.

Stan was running away.

But Barbara was still here, and I knew she would be right behind me. With a gun.

As if to confirm my racing thoughts, a shot sounded from a few yards away. Water splashed to my left as the bullet went wide of its intended target.

Me.

Sue was right. Sometimes the best plan is just to run as fast as you can.

But there was no place to go.

The woods offered some cover, but I would have to run through the entire breadth of the clearing.

The construction site was bare except for a few tiny trees in the courtyard that was to come.

There was no place to hide.

I kept moving, dodging left and right. The rain was falling harder. It turned potholes into puddles, hiding their true depth.

My boot slipped on a loose stone, turning my foot. The stiff collar of the boot protected my ankle from injury, but my foot slid out from under me, sending me toppling.

The edge of the moat appeared before me and then I was falling, sliding down the steep side to the muddy bottom.

Just like Blake.

No, I wasn't like Blake. I wasn't hurt, or dying.

And I didn't intend to be.

I heard Barbara panting at the edge of the moat above me as I cowered behind one of the piers for the temporary footbridge.

I was safe for the moment but she would spot me any second. I couldn't hide behind the pillar forever.

Barbara had used whatever was at hand to kill Blake. I had to do the same. Use whatever was available to keep her from killing me.

A bullet pinged off the pier on my right.

This was getting to be a habit — getting shot at. I didn't like it.

Standing still made me an easier target.

The sides of the moat were too steep to climb quickly, and they were slick from the pouring rain.

I ran again, splashing through the accumulating rainwater in the bottom of the moat.

My mind raced as fast as my feet. I had to find some way to fight back. Otherwise I would run until I was exhausted and then Barbara would find me and finish me.

She would have me and my car, and all the time she needed.

I would disappear again. Only this time I would never be found. This time I would disappear for good.

This time my mom would lose her house.

Anger burned hot in my chest. I would not let this woman hurt me or the people I loved.

Use whatever was at hand.

Barbara ran along the rim of the moat, her strides easily keeping pace with my frantic race along the bottom.

I followed the curve of the channel toward the back of the site. We had worked back there earlier in the autumn.

Installing sprinklers.

Sprinkler controls that would be impossible to see in the dark and the rain.

Whatever was at hand.

I put on a fresh burst of speed, forcing Barbara to increase her pace to keep up with me.

She fired another shot, missing me but breaking loose a miniature landslide just ahead of me.

I leaped over the small mound, racing toward the camouflaged sprinkler control.

I forced my legs faster. My breath came in gasps, sucking in raindrops with the oxygen my body craved.

We had to be close.

From above, a scream and a curse were followed by the solid *whump* of a tall, well-muscled body hitting the mud. A wave of muddy water splashed over the edge of the moat.

Followed by the solid *thunk* of something metal.

The gun.

She had dropped the gun.

I heard movement above me and looked up just in time to see Barbara slide over the edge of the moat. I stepped back quickly and she landed at my feet.

I didn't know if she had been injured by her fall and her slide into the moat, and I didn't care.

I didn't have a lot of sympathy for people who shot at me.

And somewhere in the muck was a gun. One I didn't want her to find again.

Barbara stirred, trying to lever herself to her feet. I jumped in the middle of her back, knocking her off-balance. She fell back on her face, frantically struggling to keep her mouth and nose out of the water.

I tried not to imagine Blake struggling the same way and failing. His injuries had killed him, but not before he fell in the water.

Where Barbara had left him to die.

I sat across her back, my weight keeping her down.

She managed to turn her head and noisily sucked a deep breath of air.

337

Now what? I needed something to tie her up.

"Georgie? Where are you?"

Sean's voice had never sounded better.

"Down here," I called. "I could use some help."

Sean's face swam out of the rain at the edge of the moat. He shone a flashlight on the two of us. "What the hell are you doing down there?"

"Catching the woman who killed Blake Weston." There was a definite note of triumph in my voice. I'd earned it.

"I need something to tie her up," I continued. "And I need the sheriff."

CHAPTER 31

I stood next to the Beetle, wrapped in a blanket from the sheriff's patrol car. My coveralls were drenched and rain and mud had soaked through to my long johns and underwear.

There was not a dry spot on my entire body.

With the wet came the cold, and I shivered with my body's effort to warm itself.

Deputy Carruthers took another blanket from his car and draped it on top of the first one. I nodded my thanks, though it didn't make me any warmer.

"We'll be heading back to the office in just a minute," he said by way of apology. "The crew's out there now, looking for the gun. And the sheriff thinks there might be a way for the lab to connect Mrs. Parks to the lead pipe that was the murder weapon."

He glanced over his shoulder to where Barbara Parks stood, hands bound behind her back by the plastic zip tie Sean had found in his tool box. Rain poured over her uncovered head, flattening her waves of red hair into stringy wisps.

She wasn't turning any heads now.

I wanted to correct him. Tell him that the pipe was galvanized steel, not lead. Nobody had used lead pipe in decades. I was a plumber. I knew these things.

But my teeth were chattering so fast I couldn't form more than a word or two.

Carruthers gave me a sympathetic look. "Let's get you in the car, okay?" He helped me into the front seat of the sheriff's idling cruiser, and turned the heater on high. "Just a couple more minutes."

I watched through the streaming rain on the windshield as another deputy helped Carruthers put Barbara Parks in the backseat of the second car.

Heat poured from the vents. My teeth slowed their clicking. I hunched over in the bulky cocoon of blankets and tried to untie my boots.

My fingers were clumsy from the chill, but eventually I got the knots loose and pushed the boots off my feet, followed by the two pair of soaked wool socks.

I shoved my feet against the floor vent, anxious for every bit of heat I could get.

The socks began to fill the car with the scent of wet wool, but I didn't care if it meant I could get warm again.

Sheriff Mitchell opened the door and sat behind the wheel. The heat washed over him, instantly bringing sweat to his brow. Without a word, he pulled off his leather jacket, Smokey-the-Bear hat, and fleece-lined gloves.

He looked at me and held out the gloves. They were too big, but they were still warm from him wearing them. I slid my clumsy hands into their depths, grateful for any source of heat.

"Carruthers swears he knows how to handle that stick shift," he said as he slipped the cruiser in reverse. "He'll take it home for you, and bring the keys back to the station."

I opened my mouth, but I was still shivering and talking took concentration. He didn't pause long enough for me to get a word out.

"Sue said she has a key to your house. She'll bring you some dry clothes to the station so you can get cleaned up, but I need you to give me a statement.

"And this time I want you to stay and sign the blasted thing."

A weak chuckle escaped from my cocoon.

The sheriff shot me a quick glance before turning his eyes back to the road.

He shook his head, a gesture of disgust or resignation, I wasn't sure which. "You keep getting involved with murder investigations, Georgie. It's not healthy."

He called me Georgie. That was a good sign that I was out from under suspicion at least.

"Y-you're telling m-m-me?" I chattered. "I t-truly do n-not like getting shot at!" My mouth was working a little better, and I went on. "Now that's a bad habit I definitely want to break."

His mouth twitched, and I was sure this time it was amusement. "You should make that your number one New Year's resolution," he said. "And I suggest you start early this year."

Sue met us at the station with an armload of warm clothes, clean undies, and a giant towel. The sheriff shooed the deputies out of their locker room, allowing me to use the tiny shower in privacy.

I spent the rest of the morning and most of the afternoon answering questions and filling the sheriff in on what I'd learned from Stan Fischer and both of the Parkses.

Some of which was even true.

The sheriff had been on the phone with

342

the San Francisco Police since Sean's first call. Richard Parks was picked up at the Samurai Security office. He was being held in the hospital ward of the San Francisco jail until they sorted out his involvement. The official diagnosis was severe shock.

Personally, I'd have called it a broken heart.

Sheriff Mitchell issued an all-points bulletin for Stan Fischer and the rented Lincoln. They expected to have him in custody soon.

The sheriff ushered me into the same bare room where we'd met before. But this time he had a deputy bring in a small sofa from his office. "Lay down if you want to," he said. "Things are kind of busy right now, so it might take a bit before the statement is ready to sign."

I wasn't happy with his instructions and it must have shown on my face.

"I'll stop back in a few minutes and bring you up-to-date."

I sat. The sofa was well worn. The springs sagged a little, like the way a pair of worn-in shoes mold to your feet.

Maybe waiting wasn't so bad.

I was resting my eyes when the door opened and the sheriff returned, rolling his leather desk chair in front of him. He rolled the chair up next to the little sofa, and dropped a stack of typed pages on the desk.

"You can take your time reading those over, just in case we missed anything. Then you can sign them and get out of here.

"Sue said she'd come get you as soon as I called. She's on her way over now."

Thank heaven for Sue. Not everyone is lucky enough to have a friend who would close their business and drop everything to bail them out.

"I suppose you'd like an update," the sheriff said, settling into his chair. "Mr. Fischer was picked up before he got to Salem. I guess he thought he could just drive the rental car all the way to San Francisco.

"We don't know everything yet, but it looks like your Mrs. Parks was a very busy lady."

The sheriff had pieced together the story from what Stan told him, and what the San Francisco P.D. had found out in a few hours of investigation. It seems there were a lot of people around Samurai that had a *lot* to say about Mrs. Barbara Parks.

According to the sheriff, Barbara Parks and Stan had known each other for several years. He'd met her when she was an intern in his lawyer's office. When I left San

Francisco, he'd introduced her to Blake, in hopes of distracting him.

It hadn't worked out.

But Barbara was smart and ambitious and she recognized the potential at Samurai Security. She met Richard Parks at a company function she attended with Blake, and when her relationship with Blake fizzled she set her sights on Richard.

Who, by the way, most certainly *did* have my job. A job Barbara was sure he would lose if I came back to Samurai.

When she found out Blake had run into me, she called Stan. The two of them had flown to Portland and Stan arranged to meet Blake at the job site.

Stan claimed Barbara grabbed the pipe and smashed Blake in the midsection. She didn't deny it, but she also hadn't spoken a single word since her arrest.

The sheriff said he hoped they could get some forensic evidence off the pipe. At least *he* didn't call it a lead pipe, which earned him points in my book.

Richard, before he collapsed, swore he knew nothing. I had seen the timid, insecure boy lurking beneath the surface when we had talked at Lucy's Diner. I told the sheriff I thought that was probably true.

He nodded as though making a mental

note, but he didn't take out his notebook or his recorder. The conversation we were having was probably way off the record.

"What about the buyout?" I asked. The damage to my reputation, even with people I never expected to see again, weighed heavily on me. I wanted to clear my name.

"We're still checking on that. The accountant at Samurai says there was a substantial payment booked at the time you left. It'll take some time to dig back in the records and figure out exactly what happened."

He smiled slowly. "Don't tell anyone I said so, but it sounds like these people are going to owe you some serious money when this is all cleared up."

Serious money sometime in the future didn't salvage my reputation. But the truth would, and that meant more than the money. Besides, if Samurai was in financial trouble, there might not be any money to be had. Serious or not.

"Thanks, Sheriff."

"You're welcome. But let's not make a habit of this, shall we? It's putting a serious cramp on my social life."

I smiled and sat forward. Moving sent several tendrils of pain through parts of my body, reminding me of the bruises I'd seen while I was changing. I was going to be sore for a while, but I knew how to deal with it.

"No more interference. Promise."

He grinned, and laid a pen on the table with the papers. "Just sign this, would you, so we can get you out of here?"

When I was through, Sue and Wade were both waiting in the reception area for me. This time they didn't appear to be fighting.

Wade helped me into the front seat of Sue's SUV, and climbed in the backseat.

Sue drove out of the lot and turned the wrong way.

"What — ?"

"Relax," Wade said soothingly over my shoulder. "We promised your mother we'd bring you by to see her. It was the only way we could keep her from camping out in the sheriff's office and raising six kinds of Cain."

I surrendered. I had planned to visit Mom anyway. Maybe this was for the best. Quick, before I changed my mind.

One complication: Gregory was sitting in Mom's living room when we arrived. I would have to find a way to talk to her alone.

That was easier than I thought. After I had reassured everyone that I would be just fine with a little rest and a decent meal, Mom motioned me to follow her into the kitchen.

Back to normal, helping Mom in the kitchen. Maybe I could find a way to tell her what I needed to while we worked.

But there wasn't any food to prepare. She just wanted to talk to me in private.

"Georgie, I am so glad you're safe. I have to admit" — she choked up a little, genuine concern thickening her voice — "I was really worried that the sheriff thought you had actually hurt that man.

"I knew you couldn't have; you couldn't hurt a fly. You used to carry spiders outside so your dad wouldn't smash them."

"Thanks, Mom. And thanks for posting my bail. I didn't want you to have to do that, but I appreciate that you did."

"You're welcome." Her eyes were moist, and I hated where I was going to take this conversation. "I think we're getting along better these days, don't you, Georgie?"

I nodded, hating myself for the words that waited for an opening, an opportunity to ruin her day. Couldn't it wait just a little longer? Couldn't I let her have this one afternoon?

If I did, it would never get said.

"I think maybe we are, Mom." I drew in a deep breath and prepared to smash the fragile truce.

"I wanted you to be the first to know."

Mom rushed in before I could speak. She held out her hand — her left hand — and wiggled her fingers.

There, on the third finger where she had worn my father's simple solitaire and gold band, was a diamond big enough to choke on.

Which is exactly what I did.

Mom rushed over to me and patted my back. Maybe a little harder than was absolutely necessary.

When the coughing fit passed and I could once again breathe — and speak — I managed to croak out, "What?"

Not the most brilliant reply, but Mom hardly noticed.

"Gregory proposed last night," she said, blushing. I didn't want to know what there was about his proposal that made her blush. Ever.

"I want you to be my maid of honor," she said. "Of course, most girls your age it would be matron of honor, but since you're still not married . . ."

She let her rebuke trail off, but the dig wasn't lost on me. In my mid-thirties and still not married. It was a disgrace.

How much of Gregory's proposal was based on love, and how much was based on Mom's finances? Was he like Blake? Did I even know how Blake really felt?

And if I wasn't sure about Blake, how could I be absolutely sure about Gregory?

But I did know about his financial problems. Even if I couldn't tell Mom, or have her find out how I knew.

"I'd be thrilled to be your maid of honor, Mom."

I hugged her, looking over her shoulder at my crossed fingers.

CHAPTER 32

Wade drove me home.

The Beetle was in the driveway, carefully locked up. When I opened the front door I found an envelope from the sheriff's department that had been dropped through the old mail slot.

Inside was the Beetle key, and a note.

"Sounds like she needs a valve adjustment. Call me at the station and we can set up a time next week. It'll take me about fifteen minutes.

"Carruthers."

The station phone number was printed neatly at the bottom of the paper.

I chuckled and stuck the note to the refrigerator with an Airedale-shaped magnet. Nice to know somebody who knew how to care for my old Beetle. It might be a relic, but it was mine.

"Georgie?" Wade slid out a kitchen chair, and motioned for me to sit across from him.

I perched on the edge of the chair. Something in Wade's voice had my tired brain going in circles.

"This has been a crazy week for you, hasn't it?"

I nodded, waiting to see what he said next.

"Do you miss all the computer stuff? Everyone from down there kept saying how good you were." Wade stood up, as though he couldn't face me as he asked the next question.

"Are you ever tempted to go back?"

"Back there?" I asked, caution slowing my words. "Or back to the computer work?"

He shrugged. "Either. Both."

Trust. I was learning to trust. That meant telling him the truth. I swallowed hard.

"Back to San Francisco? Absolutely not. I don't ever want to work that many hours or under that much stress. No."

"But? There's a *but* in there, Georgie." He looked down at me from a couple feet away.

"But I did enjoy the work itself. The things I was able to accomplish. Yeah, I miss that sometimes."

"And you got sucked back in, didn't you?"

My turn to shrug. "A little, I guess."

"Then maybe you aren't really as through with it as you thought. Is that possible?"

The thought unnerved me. I had a new

life, and the old one was gone. Or was it?

Wade looked at me, and a grin spread across his face.

"You're not sure, are you? I can see it in your eyes. You're wondering if maybe it's still there."

"So what are you so amused about? You look like you have some wonderful answer to all my problems."

I crossed my arms and scowled at him. How could he look so cheery when he was talking about messing my life up again?

"You're going to have to look at your options, Georgie. Maybe you need to be doing something with the talent you have.

"Do you remember what Chris Knight said in the movie the other night?"

Huh? *Real Genius*? What did that have to do with this?

I shook my head. Wade pulled me out of the chair, and tilted my chin up to look in his eyes.

"Your favorite movie and you don't remember? Georgie, you have to at least consider the alternatives. You have a real gift. Like he said, 'It's a moral imperative.' "

My lips twitched as I looked at Wade, grinning back at me. A smile spread slowly across my face.

"You're right," I said. "It's a moral imperative."

"Got it right the first time," Wade said, rewarding my answer with a kiss.

PLUMBING TIPS

TIP 1: If you need to find a leak in a pipe, pour some peppermint extract into the nearest drain or water input. Follow your nose to the leak.

TIP 2: When the temperature falls, protect your pipes from freezing with these suggestions:

- Leave a trickle of water running from each faucet;
- Use a heat lamp beamed at exposed pipes;
- Wrap uninsulated pipes with insulating tape, foam, heating wires, or even newspapers;
- Leave an open door between heated and unheated rooms.

TIP 3: There are several choices when unclogging a shower drain. Plungers are the first option. Though they aren't always effective, they're worth a try. If that doesn't work, use a plumber's snake to try and clear the trap. A last resort before calling a pro? No, not a harsh chemical cleaner — try a garden hose. Attach the hose to an outdoor faucet (or an indoor faucet, using a threaded adapter), push the hose deep into the drain and pack towels or rags around the opening, then turn the water on in short, hard bursts to clear the drain. Just don't leave the hose in the drain, as a sudden drop in water pressure could siphon sewage back into your fresh water supply.

TIP 4: If you're looking for a toilet tank leak, and you can't tell if the toilet is leaking around the tank bolts, try adding food coloring to the water in the tank. Wait about an hour, then touch the tips of the bolts with a white tissue. If you see color on the tissue, there's a leak. If not, it's just condensation.

When you have a condensation problem, it's usually the result of cold water in the tank and warm, moist air. The resulting condensation, or "sweating," can encourage mildew, and loosen floor tile. Left unattended it can damage subflooring. One easy solution is to empty the tank and glue foam rubber pads to the inside of the tank as insulation. If that doesn't work, it's time to call a pro to install a tempering valve, which will mix hot and cold water when filling the tank, to avoid the temperature differential that causes the sweating.

TIP 5: Water heaters are a wonderful invention. Just ask anyone who has had one quit working in the middle of a shower. But because they operate on either gas or electricity, they are a potential source of trouble. Most problems are signaled by water that is either too hot or not hot enough. But if you hear rumbling — a sign of overheating — or have steam or boiling water come out of the valve or hot water faucets, shut the heater off IMMEDIATELY to avoid a dangerous situation.

A noisy water heater is often the result of scale and sediment buildup in the tank. The simplest solution is to turn off the heater and drain the tank to clear out the sediment. In an electric heater it may also indicate scale buildup on the element. If the element has scale buildup, you can remove the element, soak it in vinegar, and scrape off the scale.

TIP 6: There are three main causes of noisy

pipes: loose pipes, water logged air chambers, and water pressure that's too high. Here are some suggestions for dealing with each of them.

Banging is usually caused by loose pipes. Loose pipes are an easy fix, if they're accessible. For concealed pipes — inside walls, ceilings, and floors — you may want to consider professional help. But if you can reach a pipe you can anchor it to thwart its noise-making potential.

Pipe straps should be placed every six to eight feet on horizontal runs, and every eight to ten feet on vertical runs. If the pipes bang when you turn on the water, try adding straps, or cushioning the pipes with a rubber blanket, or both. If it's a plastic pipe, be sure to leave room for expansion. And never use a galvanized strap on a copper pipe. The two metals do not play well together.

Hot water pipes may squeak. Hot water can expand the pipe, causing it to move in its strap and the friction may make the pipe squeak. Cushioning the pipe should help solve the problem.

Hammering happens when the water is turned off quickly. When the water slams to a stop it can cause a hammering sound. Check for loose pipes and treat accordingly.

If the cause isn't loose pipes, it may be water-logged air chambers, the lengths of pipe behind fixtures and appliances. These pipes are intended to hold a cushion of air to absorb the shock when the water is shut off. They can become filled with water and lose the ability to do their job.

It's pretty easy to reset the air chambers. Just turn off the water to the system at the main shutoff valve. Then open all the faucets and let the system drain completely. When the system is drained, close the faucets and turn the main valve back on. The air chambers should refill with air. If that doesn't work, check to see if your water pressure is too high (above eighty pounds per square inch {psi}).

You can install a pressure-reducing valve to deal with the problem. Or call in a plumber like Georgie or Barry if you don't want to tackle that job yourself.